MW01126698

The Uninvited

Vol I

By Mike Evans

Mike Evans

Dedicated to my wife and children, who are always ready to put up with one of my crazy ideas. Always supportive of my writing. I love you all. Also to my fans and readers this has been an amazing year!

****

The Uninvited is a work of fiction By Mike Evans. All of the characters contained herein are fictional, and all similarities to persons living or dead are purely coincidental.
This text cannot be copied or duplicated without author or publisher written permission from the author.

This eBook is licensed for your personal enjoyment upon purchase. This eBook may not be traded or sold to other people. If you want to share this book with others, please purchase an additional copy. If you are reading this but did not purchase it, please return it to where you got it from. Thanks for respecting this author's work.

Please don't forget to leave a REVIEW! Authors rely on _you_, the reader, to help widen their audience through word of mouth and feedback. Getting stars and good reviews helps us on our way.
Thank you for reading!

Editing Donelle Pardee Whiting
Special thanks to Christy Thornbrugh for reading it raw, and the proofreading done by Karen Dziegiel & Rosa Thomas-Mcbroom!
Cover by Lisa Vasquez Stock Images: Shutterstock and Marcus J. Ranum

© 2016 Mike Evans, All Rights Reserved

A quick note from the author, if you enjoyed this please head to Amazon to REVIEW or give it a star rating please

Mike Evans Fan Club Page Facebook
https://www.facebook.com/groups/1523345561293296/
Mike Evans Author Website
http://mevansm01.wix.com/mikeevansauthor
Contact Email
m.evansauthor@gmail.com
Mike Evans on Amazon
http://www.amazon.com/Mike-Evans/e/B00IQ9Z75A

Mike Evans

Books by Mike Evans

The Orphans Series
The Orphans: Origins Vol I
Surviving the Turned Vol II (The Orphans Series)
Strangers Vol III (The Orphans Series)
White Lie Vol IV (The Orphans Series)
Civil War Vol V (The Orphans Series)

Zombies and Chainsaws
Zombies and Chainsaws 1
Dark Roads (Zombies and Chainsaws 2)

The Rising Series
Deal with the Devil Book 1

Gabriel Series
Gabriel: Only one gets out alive
Pitch Black (Gabriel Book 2)
Body Count (Gabriel Book 3)

The Uninvited Series
The Uninvited Book 1
The Stranger Book II of The Uninvited series coming soon

Buried: Broken oaths

Chapter 1

Summer of 1970

Mary walked through the house checking the different rooms. She couldn't find her son anywhere and had searched every inch of the house. Mary saw her husband Paul and asked, "Hey, honey, have you seen your son?"

"My son? What did he do this time?"

"I just haven't seen him in a while, and I don't like him having too much free time. You know as well as I do how much trouble he can get into."

Paul got up from his chair, and set down his daily paper. "Fine, we'll go see what he is up to then. Will that make you happy?"

"A million dollars would make me happy, Paul. Then we'd have enough to be able to figure out what is wrong with him."

Paul opened the back door and they stopped short. "Oh my God, Paul. He...he's done it again, but it looks worse this time."

"Just wait here, honey. Let me go talk to him. Hey, buddy, are you doing okay out here?"

The boy looked up, smiling, a distant look in his eyes. "Hi, Daddy. Look, look what I did, dad. There was a stray cat. I sent him to Heaven."

"Son you need to remember what we told you, that it isn't your job to do that. You can't do that, son. You are going to be taken away from us if you can't stop doing that. Do you think you can stop; do you need help?"

"Why would I want to stop? I like it, Daddy."

Chapter 2

Thursday, May 2000

Steven waved to the security guard as he drove out of the Ford plant and started his hour ride home. He'd been taking this route for a decade, and it seemed to get a little longer every day. Steven flipped through the radio stations ignoring the news; he'd seen plenty of bad times in his life, he did not need the assistance of others to tell him how bad the world was.

Steven exited the interstate and hung a right heading for his property. He loved living in the middle of nowhere. The peace and quiet was something they'd never had in the city, and they took the first chance they'd had to purchase property in the boonies. They ended up right next to a state park and had never regretted the decision.

He drove slowly, seeing the reflective lights of a car on the shoulder of the road. When he saw the Chevy ribbon flashing off the car he laughed to himself. He knew damn well Fords could end up on the side of the road too, but it was no different than a buddy's football team losing and yours prevailing.

He slowed the truck down, leaning across the seat divider and rolling down the old crank window. He yelled, "Hey, buddy, you need a hand there? I'm pretty handy as long as it ain't too complicated."

The man stood holding the tire iron, and when he turned around Steven yelled, unable to comprehend what he was seeing. Steven squinted trying to see the man better. The truck light from his cab was not enough to make the man out well. All that he could see was what looked like a white china doll mask that was missing the eyes and had a black cross running down the forehead.

Steven mouthed "what in the fuck." The man started walking toward him and began raising the tire iron. Steven, knowing it'd do little good as old as the truck was, pushed the truck's gas pedal down until it was touching the floor. The truck raced off, skidding on the gravel road. Steven let off the gas when he heard a heavy thud on the side of the truck knowing the man had just struck its side with the tire iron. He let the truck coast for a minute until he had it under control and when he pulled into the driveway of his home accelerated yet again until he came to a skidding stop in front of the home.

Steven practically fell out of the truck as he moved a state of panic. His wife Christy was sitting in her recliner watching her husband fall to the ground only to bear crawl until he was standing and running. She was sewing up a pair of his work pants and stabbed herself with the needle when she became alarmed at her husband's antics. She tried to make the most out of what they had so when it came time to pay for the propane for the winter they would have the money they needed to help keep their farm warm throughout the winter.

"Ow, son of a bitch!" she yelled, and she immediately stuck her finger in her mouth, sucking on the droplet of blood.

Steven rushed through the door slamming it behind him and locking it. "You got the back door shut and locked, baby?"

She sucked on the blood and stared at him in shock. "Well, fucking hello to you too, your highness. You made me stab myself god damn it. Do you know how much that hurts?"

Steven pulled out his pocketknife. "I got my pocket knife on me if you need me to amputate it, sweetie."

Christy, still sucking frantically at her finger, held up a pair of scissors taking a break from her wound. "You need me to amputate something for you Steven; because I can assure you, honey, it would be my pleasure."

Steven quickly put away his knife. Christy said, "Is there a reason you are acting like a damn maniac? Did you need something Steven, or were you just trying to get my nerves all rattled?"

"No, I got a reason believe it or not; there was some weirdo out on the highway to our road. He had his truck pulled over to the side of the road and-"

"Damn it Steven, how many times do I gots to tell you that just because someone's car breaks down on the side of the road it doesn't mean that they are some-"

"Christ, would you shut up! I saw a weirdo, yes I do mean weirdo, woman. He was crouched down by his tire and, me being the good Samaritan I am, asked if he needed to get any assistance. When he stood up he was holding a tire iron and had a white creepy ass mask on with a black cross down the middle of it. Now what do you have to say?"

"So you rushed home and that is what leads us up to right now, huh?"

Steven nodded his head. Still panting, he said, "So do you have the back door locked or not?"

She shook her head, "No, I wasn't expecting to hear

that believe it or not. But tell you what. Why don't you go ahead and take care of that task yourself and from there you need to call down and see if you can get ahold of Sheriff Laughlin and see if he'll come down and check out the man."

Steven nodded, saying more to himself that it was a good idea, and headed towards the back of the house, flicking on every light he could on the way there, trying to make the house look as uninviting as possible.

When he plucked the phone off the wall he listened for the dial tone but heard nothing. He instantly ran through every conversation he'd had with his friends over the year and the repeated speech of you all need to get yourselves a damn cell phone and it wouldn't matter no such way if you was coming or going. The two of them had been adamant once you gave into one of them there phones you never went back, and the modern technology age wasn't something they were hungry to try.

Steven yelled, "Hey, baby, you had any problems with the phone today? You make any calls on it?"

"No, you been at work all day I don't have shit to say to anyone but you and that's just because you live here."

Steven brought the phone down ready to smash it but refrained and opened the kitchen's rear door slowly. He peered around, shining a light on the side of the house where he knew the phone line ran down it and saw it was separated. He shined the light around his property. He yelled, "Zero, Zero, get your ass in the house now!"

The dog did not bark back, and he yelled to Christy, "Baby, when's the last time you seen the dog today?"

"That ignorant shit went out when you left for work

this morning and the last time I saw him he was running like a bat out of hell after a group of rabbits that he looked like he was going to give a run for their money."

He went across the property one last time stopping near the barn when he saw what looked like a man in dark overalls disappearing behind it. He squinted in the dark, but it was too late and the figure was gone. Steven shut the door tight, locking the knob and the bolt. He said, "Go get my shotgun, baby, hurry up now!"

"Well, then I'm gonna need to borrow your damn truck then."

Steven collapsed against the wall. He remembered his friend Joey stopping by to tell him he needed to borrow it so that he could get rid of some pests around the property. Steven knew he needed something else and began running through the house towards Christy.

"Okay so I don't want you to freak out, but I'm pretty sure that asshole from the highway just walked back behind the barn."

Christy pushed up from the chair still sucking on her finger. When they looked out the kitchen window, they saw the man in the mask standing beneath the one light that hung from the garage. Steven opened the door and Christy stopped him from going out.

"This woman just saved your life dickhead. You'd better thank God himself that I'm not coming out there, or I'm gonna put the hurt on you damn it."

The man didn't falter. He didn't move. He simply stood there swaying back and forth. Steven said, "You get out of here and you do it now damn it, do you hear me, boy?"

The man shook his head no and threw something above him shattering the light on the barn and sending himself into pitch black. Christy jumped a foot, grabbing Steven and yelling, "What the fuck is wrong with that guy?"

Steven, never took his eyes off the now empty spot, "A lot!"

Steven closed the door, locking it tightly. He peered out of the blinds and watched as the uninvited man started to walk slowly towards them. Christy gripped his shoulder shaking him. "What are we gonna do, baby? We can't call the cops, and he looks fucked up five ways to Sunday. What the hell is with the mask?"

"I don't have a damn clue, honey. Maybe it is a good thing that he doesn't want us to know what he looks like, and that he is planning on just being creepy and then leaving."

They watched the man for a moment and saw him slide a hand behind his back. When it came back, it looked like he had an extension of his arm that went on forever. When the man turned to the side, they saw his arm extension was really a two sided axe head. This did little to make the two of the Thornbrugh's feel any better. Steven looked around the kitchen, then grabbed a chef knife off the chopping block and handed it to Christy. He gave her a quick hug and said, "I want you to get upstairs, baby."

"Steven Dale Thornbrugh if you think for one god damned minute I'm going to just go upstairs and hide then you are-"

Steven brushed the side of her face, spun her around, and gave her a slap on the ass she would not soon forget. She said, "Jesus Christ save my ass would you?"

Steven did the sign of the cross saying, "I am trying to save it, baby. I am. I promise."

The back door started to rattle and Steven screamed, "Get the fuck off my property you piece of shit. I'm calling the cops right goddamn now!"

Steven walked forward to move the curtain. The man in the mask was standing there staring directly into the window. Steven yelled, "I'm calling the police you piece of shit!"

The man pointed to where the wire was hanging and shook his head slowly. He stopped wiggling the doorknob and backed away out of view. Steven wished he had his shotgun right now more than anything. He moved back from the window knowing the man had called his bluff. He shut the kitchen door behind him and slid a chair in front of it hoping that it would be enough if the man came through the kitchen. He went to triple check the front door and that was when the lights went out.

A voice shrieked from upstairs. Steven screamed, "Christy, are you okay, baby? Is he up there? Did he get you?"

"No, he didn't get me. Christ, you think I'd be screaming like some dumb bitch, or do you think I'd be saying, honey get your good for nothing ass up here now! I think that we know the answer to that."

Steven went to say something when the front door began to wiggle. He looked at it and whoever was on the outside started ramming a shoulder into it.

"You break that door down, and I can promise you I'm gonna break your fucking head open you crazy son of a bitch!"

The door stopped thudding and Steven backed away from it, putting a hand to his chest to feel his heart rate. He held out his hands, realizing he'd sent Christy upstairs with the knife and had picked up nothing he could use to make his threats come to life but his own bare shaking, hands. Steven was confident from the size of the stranger that he could literally rip him in half if he wanted to. He looked around wildly in the living room until the fireplace, which seemed to be calling him with its red embers glowing in the dark now showed off the tools he had hanging next to it. Steven gripped the poker on it and liked its weight; he selected it because of its sharpness and weight. He prayed it would be the weapon to save their lives if it came to that.

Christy yelled from the upstairs, "Baby, what's going on down there, did he leave?"

Steven didn't answer. He walked towards the front bay window, trying to see out, but could see nothing. He didn't dare touch the shades, thinking if the man had a gun he could simply shoot into the now equally dark house and blow his head off. Steven jumped when a thud hit the long picture window. He wasn't stupid and was aware of just how little it would take to break through the old thing. He moved forward slowly and used the fire poker to separate the curtain. Steven leaned closer trying to see what it was. He pulled a Zippo from his pants and flicked the lighter open one handed and ran his thumb down the flint wheel. Each time he had a reason to light it, he always missed his smoking days.

He held the light closer to the window and all he could see was a deep red smudge making its way down that he feared was blood. He could not see the man anymore.

He listened waiting for him to jump back out and scare the shit out of him again; unfortunately, he didn't have to wait long. The masked man stepped out from his cover off to the side of the window and into plain view. He brought up one hand and put his index finger to what was dirtying the window. He drew a smiley face on it and disappeared back into the black of night.

Steven realized he was pretty damn easy to see holding the damn lighter and flicked shut the top, killing the oxygen. He looked at the smiley face, still trying to think of what it was, when a shadow formed from a distance and got larger and larger. It was all black by the time it was only inches from him. The man was running towards the window with something large in his hands. He heaved the object, and it soared through the air, crashing hard into the window and breaking it open. Steven fell backwards, tripping over a footstool hitting the floor hard and losing his fire poker as it skidded away under a chair. "Oh fuck me."

Steven hit his lighter again, this time not caring about the man but wanting to verify his worst thoughts. When he struck the lighter, he saw the mangled, bloody body of his bird hunting dog Zero, lying on the floor decapitated and gone. He crawled up next to him rubbing his head on his fur smelling the familiar smell that he complained of daily when the dog would crawl up on the couch.

Steven screamed aloud, "You son of a bitch. I'm gonna fucking kill you, do you hear me god damn you! You don't touch a man's dog!"

Christy came back from her hiding spot upstairs to look down into the living room and saw her husband, the broken window, and Zero lying in front of him and had a piece of her heart break instantly. She said, "Honey, you okay down there?"

Steven, now on the verge of tears, had snot running from his nose and was doing his best not to have an emotional breakdown of epic proportions.

"Jesus woman do I fucking look okay? He got Zero. He got my fucking dog! Who goes after a fucking dog?" He stood, turning around to look up to her, and yelled, "You get back into your damn room and I want you to lock it and stick something heavy in front of it, baby. Do it now!"

This time Christy screamed, and it filled the old country house, pouring out of the broken window. "Baby, behind you!"

Steven turned around to see the stranger standing at the broken window again. This time he ducked his massive frame beneath the broken glass, gripping each side of the window frame with heavy-duty work gloves that would protect his hands and pulled himself up, casting a shadow that would have engulfed Steven had it not been for the flame. Steven backed up a few feet, diving for the chair where he'd heard his one and only weapon go sliding beneath.

Christy stood atop the staircase, frozen and gripping the handrail, unable to move. She watched as Steven rushed for the chair. The man moved smoothly and not in a hurry seeming to be not scared in the least of the two. Steven felt a short moment of victory when he grasped the golden poker and pulled it out. He went to roll over and as he did a burst of pain exploded through his leg. Steven used the zippo to see what it was and could see the man holding firmly to a meat hook with the business end sticking through Steven's calf. Steven cried out in pain and Christy muffled her screams, trying unsuccessfully to remain silent as she watched her own personal horror show taking place.

Steven lost the poker when the man broke skin, sending a surge of pain through his leg. He tried to keep the man from dragging him outside but could do little to stop him. Steven, no slouch himself, knew that he looked like a runt compared to this behemoth of a man. He kicked with his good leg at the stranger's legs. Steven got it just right sending one man's leg behind the other and throwing him off balance. The man fell, hitting his head on a side table before collapsing to the ground. Christy yelped, "Oh my god, move, baby, move, get your poker. Get your poker, and kill that fucker!"

Steven tried to stand and realized his left leg wasn't good for shit with the meat hook through it. He gripped it and knew it wasn't going anywhere without a professional lovingly removing it; one who he hoped would be equipped with painkiller drugs, and anesthesia. He stumbled on a knee looking more like a gorilla moving through his living room than a man. Steven could tell he was seriously injured as the blood loss was beginning to slow down his thinking. He shook his head and clenched the poker. He used it to get up from the ground with its help, and hobbled towards the man quickly.

Christy yelled, "See who it is?"

Steven yelled, "I don't give a shit who it is, that's going to be for the coroner and police to figure out."

"What baby?"

"I'm going to kill the mother fucker. We can call the police later."

Steven got within skull striking distance of the man and the poker whistled through the air as he swung at the man's masked head. When it was within inches of striking him the stranger's right hand came from nowhere gripping it. The man sat up, shaking off his own injuries and placed his other hand on the meat hook, pulling it as hard as he could and yanking it free from Steven's leg. A geyser worth of blood sprayed out in every direction and Steven collapsed to the ground screaming in agony.

Steven released his grip on the poker and fell to the floor. The man took it and the meat hook and got back to his feet. He took the meat hook down in one long swing, sticking it through Steven's shoulder this time. Steven screamed again, clawing at it, cursing every word he knew, and a few new ones, the man to let go. The man did not listen to anything, he simply started his walk back outside with Steven in tow. He did not drag him across the broken window, instead going to the front door, opening it and disappearing into the dark.

Christy, watching all of this in horror, had no way of knowing what was happening outside. She ran to their room, getting a Maglite, and shined it from the second story down on the man who seemed oblivious to the beam of light. Steven was clawing at the man, but with the position he was facing, straight up being dragged backwards through dirt and gravel, it did little good to save him.

Christy had tears running freely and a burning anger she hadn't felt in decades coursing through her body. She pounded on the window hard with the light, shining it down upon them and leaving a thirty-foot silhouette of the man casting him into an even larger monster than he already was. He stopped at the barn's entrance, disappearing into the darkness. Steven lay there bleeding and trying to crawl away, but with one lame arm and leg there was no getting away. Christy wanted to go to the stairs but couldn't bring herself to leave the window.

The man appeared in the second story of the barn and stared directly across at Christy. It had taken her a minute to realize where he had gone, and then to her horror what he was doing. When the man saw the light upon him he looked up, stopping what he was doing and waving to her, and then went back to his work of lowering the large rope that hadn't been used in years, not since Steven had quit working on local farmer's tractors in the massive barn to help make ends meet.

The man disappeared again, melting back into the darkness and a moment later, he was standing next to a bloodied and exhausted Steven who, even in his now crippled state, was trying to escape. Christy watched, praying by some chance he would find a way to get away. The man let Steven crawl as he undid the rope, bringing the pulley system down with the large hook hanging from it. She beat on the window more to get his attention. He simply tilted his head to the side and waved to her.

Christy knew she was no match for him but had to do something to try to save the love of her life. She ran down the stairs, slowing for only a second as she took in so many happy memories hanging on the wall. She wasn't ignorant and knew that even if they somehow survived this night that the two of them would always be changed going forward. The false sense of trust the two of them shared

19

living in the country would be gone.

Christy barged out of the front door with the Maglite still in her hand. She hit the on button, shining it directly in the man's eyes and not wavering at all. The man quit tightening the rope around Steven and let go. He walked directly towards Christy, ignoring Steven who was still trying to escape on the ground and leaving a bloody trail behind him.

"You son of a bitch. I'm going to crack your damn head open. You messed with the wrong woman today mother fucker!"

Steven gripped the man's leg with his good hand. The man pulled a hammer out of his overalls; it looked like it might as well have been a children's tool compared to the size of the man's hand. He brought it down once into Steven's hand, the echo of his bones breaking pierced Christy's eardrums. He screamed trying to clutch it but his opposite arm was of little use to him now. His eyes began to fill with tears, ones that were shortly going to become rage.

The man continued walking to Christy, who brought the light up one time and swung it at the man's chest. His head was almost two feet higher than her delicate small frame could reach. The man gripped the flashlight with his right hand, blocking her swing, and gripped her ears bringing them and her skull down quicker than anyone could imagine possible, connecting his right knee to her nose. She felt the bones shatter beneath it and warm blood started to run down her face and into her mouth leaving a metallic taste to it.

She started to fall to the ground but the man gripped

her by the back of her shirt keeping her standing, not allowing her to fall down. He dragged her through the dirt toward her husband. Christy screamed as dragged her, "What is wrong with you?"

The stranger reached the barn near Steven. He had been thinking of her question, and when they made it there, threw her on the ground. She looked up, blood and tears now almost blinding her.

"What the hell is wrong with you?"

The man tilted his head back and forth almost suggesting he was debating what it was that they were asking. He held up his hands a foot apart, Christy snapped, "Well, what the fuck is that supposed to mean?"

Steven collapsed on the ground. He could take no more of this. "He's telling you that there is a lot wrong with him. You are wasting your breath, Christy," he whispered. "This son of a bitch is bat shit crazy, and there ain't anything that, you, or anyone else is going to be able to do about it."

The man clenched onto the meat hook hanging out of Steven's shoulder and in one violent pull ripped it from his shoulder. Steven thought the pain he experienced while being dragged out to the barn like a wet useless doll had been the worst feeling in his life. The pain that poured out of his arm now was nothing short of the most excruciating thing that he had ever felt. The pain from his shoulder radiated throughout his body.

"Fuck you, you, son of a bitch. We ain't scared of you, damn it!" Christy screamed with hatred burning in her eyes.

Steven tried to retort but was crying too intensely from the pain. The stranger knelt down next to him, patting

Steven on the head, stroking his hair into a million different sweaty directions. The man made his first noise since arriving, hushing him and caressing the side of his face. Steven looked up, even more confused, and the man continued to pat him on the head. When Steven finally thought something good might happen to him, that whatever dark world this freak was in had left, was when things got worse. Much worse.

The man stood, wiping the meat hook, and then brought it down with everything he possessed. And from the size of the man, that was something to be scared of. He stabbed the meat hook into Steven's thigh this time, twisting it so his torso and head would hang down like an animal in the barn being skinned.

"Baby, it's going to be okay, it's going to be fine. We are gonna get you help before it's too late!" Christy yelled to Steven.

The man shook his head, slowly lifting Steven with both arms as he clawed and scraped to be freed. The stranger attached the meat hook to what he had put on the barn rope and began pulling on the pulley system. Christy yelled again and this time for her trouble got a hammer to the side of the head, leaving her unconscious on the gravel.

Steven was not running out of tears but was lacking the ability to make as many as he needed to so he could shed them for what he was feeling both emotionally and physically. He stared numbly at Christy lying on the dark gravel path. Her eyes knew not where they were and Steven could see the blood pooling from the side of her head, making a path between the small rocks until it found a place to pool.

Steven tried reaching for the man as he swung but missed him. He was lifted up until he was four feet in the air, too far to reach the dirt and gravel covered driveway. The man disappeared back into the barn, and when he came out was carrying one of the extra mower blades Steven kept extras of. This one shined in the light when he came back out. He stood patiently hushing Steven and waiting for Christy to come out of her trance. When she did, Steven felt momentary relief, seeming to forever think she was gone. She was not.....at least for the moment.

When she could focus again, she stared at her husband and watched as the stranger brought the mower blade across his midsection, not hesitating or slowing down. The white flab of his belly became red instantly; blood poured down into his chest hair, dripping off his head to the ground below. Christy tried to reach for him when the man ran the blade down each side of his abdomen, leaving it open for his guts to pour out of his stomach cavity.

They fell to the ground, hitting and spreading across covering Christy. She screamed until she passed out in the gravel. A grinding feeling began to wake her. When she opened her eyes she saw the moon and the stars passing slowly above her. She tried to scream, wiggling her tongue, but she felt nothing, only a constant throbbing in her mouth. She reached a hand up to her mouth sticking her fingers in but did not feel her tongue or teeth.

When she started to try to scream the man looked down at her and dropped a tongue on her face followed by a splash worth of teeth. Fresh tears began to fall down the side of her face as he dragged her back into the house.

Chapter 3

Friday

Traci sat at her desk googling the state parks and thinking of the long three-day weekend ahead. Her coworker Brandi came up behind her seeing the webpage.

"Why, didn't you just take a half a day off like all the other slackers? You are doing about as much work as anyone."

Traci smiled, "I would but I'm out of vacation time, and we can't afford to take it unpaid right now. I know that Isaac is going to get a promotion soon. We just need to be patient for a little bit longer."

"Well, this is exactly why I am glad that I don't have college loans to worry about. What do you make, fifty cents extra an hour?"

"Well, you know what they say; it's always a waste of money to further one's education Brandi. Besides, this is an internship, so when I finish this and they see how remarkable I am I'll get a better job here and actually be able to afford take out and manicures again."

Brand held out her hands, "Yeah, it's almost like you are living like a poor person."

"Yeah, Brandi, if that meant that Isaac and I lived in a car instead of a two-bedroom apartment with a nice view. Did you need something, or were you just wasting your half of your day before our weekend starts?"

"Oh, I'm just wandering around, there's always a treat day, and well, who can pass up nacho cheese dip? It's like it should be a food group or something. So you guys going on a trip then?"

"I hope so, I'm going to try and talk Isaac into it. I have powers of persuasion that I can use to talk him into going to one of the many state parks in Missouri."

"So what does that mean, you are going to owe him a blow job for him taking you out for an entire day?"

"Jesus, Brandi, do you have like no filter?"

"Not as of the last time I checked."

"What are you doing this weekend? Three days to kill, what are you going to do?"

"I'm going to go out this weekend wearing something that will be a nice insurance policy that I will not have to pay for any drinks, and that if a bit of me needs pleasuring that I'll be able to guarantee those needs are met as well."

"Don't you want more for yourself?"

Brandi sat down on the corner of the desk, tilting her head back and forth. "Geez, so what you're really asking is if I need a relationship in my life to be complete and happy? You know as tempting as the idea of the same penis going in and out of me until the point that I have to actually work to get him hard regardless of what I do or wear just so I can get a great little four minute fucking is, I am going to pass. The fact that I can get a hot fuck one day and then on the nights I want to stay in be able to walk around my place without a boyfriend dry humping, doesn't break my heart. I'm okay with passing, thanks."

"But don't you want love? Don't you ever, you know.....get lonely?"

"I have a vibrator: I promise you I am never lonely, and I don't ever not get satisfied, unless I get a minute man. God I hate those. I mean at the least when they cum too fast you'd think that they could finger-"

"Oh my god, TMI, TMI. Brandi, my ears are going to start bleeding soon. I'm a delicate flower, or did you forget?"

Brandi laughed with a snort sending an echo of it down the row of cube city. "Oh please, Traci, I've seen you strolling in every morning with a glow that only means your toes curled in the morning. You got one of the good ones, which just means that there's one less out there for me to try and get if ever I get bored of this horrible life that I lead now."

"Well, I would say that I don't have too much to worry about in that department, whatever horror story you think that you would have if you were dating someone is the farthest thing from my mind. I've been with Isaac for four years, and I'm still yet to catch him looking around at other women or have trouble getting him ready in bed."

"Porn, Traci, its porn, and they all use it. Makes perfect sense though. But hey, this is a judgment free zone so don't worry about it. I've been known to watch a foot long from time to time."

Traci watched the computer, her face and neck growing red from embarrassment. "You know I heard that accounting catered in today. I'm not trying to get rid of you, but you know damn well that they have got the best catered food in the company."

"Well, those that get paid well get fed well. Hey, maybe they are going out for drinks. Those nerds never get laid, so I'm sure I could get a free night of drinking."

Brandi hopped off of the desk, unbuttoning her blouse a few extra than work allowed, and said, "Have fun out in the woods, Traci."

"Good luck with your free drinks and food, Brandi. Try to stay out of trouble."

She turned around, smiling. "Aim big or go home."

Traci looked at the clock, seeing the time was close enough she could sneak home and get some items prepared in case she was able to get Isaac to agree to going out this weekend. She only hoped that he could leave his work behind, and they could have some much needed time together. She knew that times had been tough with him and they were just scraping by month to month. She made a short grocery list of wines, cheeses, and snacks they could enjoy while pretending for the afternoon they had the money they needed on a daily basis. She didn't kid herself, because they'd be just as happy with screw top wine as getting the kind needed to have a corkscrew.

Chapter 4

Saturday Morning

Traci woke up early to the songs of birds sitting on the windowsill. She smiled, stretched out, and then tiptoed to the bathroom where she brushed out her dark hair and did a quick gargle. Traci sat on the toilet and began checking her phone. The weatherman predicted the day was going to be beautiful with temperatures in the seventies, a light breeze, and zero chance of rainfall. She smiled, thinking it was days like this that changed people's lives, and wondered if there was any chance of Isaac bringing up the little white box that she had found the week before when doing his laundry. She had refused to open it…for the first ten minutes anyway. She felt if she was going to go to hell that there was no way that God could judge her for this. The only thing harder was not letting on she knew, or calling to tell her mother the size of the rock could be confused with a small mountain.

She opened the door, leaving her panties and tank top on the floor; smiling, she slid back into bed and pulled the comforter back over herself. She lay there looking at the time thinking seven wasn't too early to wake Isaac to let him know about the wonderful day she'd planned for them. She'd made sure to cook the night before and had even put herself on beer duty making sure he had no reason to get in the fridge and snoop around only to see the snacks and wine she'd found at the store on the way home.

Traci watched Isaac for a minute longer looking at his eyelids and seeing that he was having some sort of pleasant dream and almost felt guilty. She was confident given the small tent coming from his half of the bed that she was going to be able to make whatever he might be dreaming about become a reality. She snuggled up close to him, not trying to be overly obvious about waking him up. When he did not stir, she started running a hand from his leg across him and up his stomach slowly missing nothing in between. He smiled as he began to wake up, still not opening his eyes.

"Traci, I can feel your nipples on the side of my chest."

Traci, being playful, said, "Oh honey, that is because I'm naked," Traci replied playfully.

He smiled bigger at this, running his left hand down her side, cupping her breast, and then checked that panties were part of this nakedness as well.

"Did you have something you needed to do?"

She kissed his cheek, wrapping a hand around him slowly going back and forth. "Well….it kind of feels to me like you might have something that you need me to do. But I wanted to ask you if you thought you might have some time for a little road trip today?"

The smile left his face, "I have some reports that I needed to work on, honey. You know that fucking promotion is just around the corner."

She stopped rubbing him and leaned his face towards hers. "Honey, eventually we are going to have a million babies running around here, and we are never going to be able to road trip or have sex freely in the morning again. Now are you sure that you couldn't be bothered by a little cruise down to one of the state parks with some wine and cheese, and maybe a repeat of this?"

He smiled, pushing up a little on to his side. "Well, it is a three day weekend right? What exactly do you mean when you are talking about a repeat?"

Traci pushed him onto his back and climbed on top of him, letting the comforter fall down around her waist as she gripped him and slowly let him enter her. Isaac rubbed his hands up and down her legs, staring at his idea of perfection. He smiled, sat up and kissed her breasts.

"So what you are saying is.....you really want to go on a road trip today?"

She kissed his neck and then licked his earlobe. "It's kind of a long drive there too, so I just hope that we don't get too bored in the car. You never know what I'm going to have to do to keep myself occupied."

Isaac laughed at this. "You might not want to say things like that though, honey."

She stopped rising her legs up and down, "What, so you'd rather me just sit on my side of the car the entire ride?"

He laughed, edging her on to keep riding him, "No, oh my good god no. I just think if I know you are going to do that every time that you get bored I'm never going to stop driving."

She pushed him back down onto the bed, bending down kissing his chest. "Fine, then I'm going to cap the drive to one blow job on the way there, and if you are good at the park then we may or may not have a reason to take a blanket to stretch out on."

He smiled at this. "What has gotten into you this morning?"

"Just happy about the weekend, and you and I both work too hard, getting out into the wilderness and just relaxing isn't going to hurt us a bit."

He could tell by the look on her face she wasn't kidding and she really did need this. He nodded his head. "You want to go for a drive, we go for a drive. There's nothing saying that I didn't work all day if I still get the shit done right? God Forbid that I take my fiancé out on a drive, right?"

This stopped her rhythm immediately. She said, "Excuse me?"

He said, "Well, it wasn't exactly how I was planning on asking you, but I can't think of a time that I've felt better recently."

He opened the nightstand drawer next to him, pulling out the box and opening it he smiled and held the ring out for her to see....for the second time. She gripped the box, holding it to her chest. Tears started to roll down the side of her face. Isaac took the box back from her, pulled the delicate looking gold band from its place, and slid it on the ring finger of her left hand, kissing her hand once it was in place.

Traci bent down, kissed him long and deep, then started moving her hips again, and did not break the kiss until the two of them finished at the same time. She whispered, "This is the happiest moment of my entire life, Isaac Hunter. I love you so much."

"You'd better, that thing cost me a-"

Traci put a finger to his lips and hushed into his ear. "Shhh, don't ruin it, baby. I love it. It's my newest and most favorite thing. I can promise you that. I love you so much it hurts, Isaac. I cannot wait until my last name matches yours. We are going to be so happy, I just know it, baby. Oh my god, do you know how many phones calls we are going to have to make?"

Isaac rubbed her back and whispered, "We will never…I mean ever, leave if you call your friends and mother now. Why don't we keep it between the two of us just for today? What is it going to hurt? You have the ring, and we are engaged. We can just enjoy being newly engaged and in love for the day."

She rolled off him, looking at her ring and smiling. "Who wants to be on the phone all day on a beautiful Saturday? I'm going to get in the shower and then I say we hit the road. Do you want to get in with me?"

Isaac rubbed her bottom. "I do, but I need a few minutes, honey. I'm not twenty anymore."

"Oh no, am I going to marry an old man?"

"You go get cleaned up and I'll meet you in a minute. I want to check a few things."

"If you end up working all morning, I'm going to hurt you, you know that right?"

"Yes, Mrs. Hunter, I sure do. I just need ten or fifteen minutes, and we are good to go. Swear to God."

She rolled off the bed, and bent down kissing him on the lips, and ran to the bathroom. She covered herself with the comforter until she reached the doorway leaving him naked on the bed. Isaac hit the remote for the news and started looking up his fantasy baseball league stats. He got up pulled on a pair of boxers and padded to the kitchen to start a pot of coffee to brew.

The news anchor on Channel 13 started the next

report, "We have breaking news to report. A family of four was found brutally murdered in their home. The police are not giving any hard details yet. This is the seventh slaying in the metro area. Police have no leads and no witnesses. Detective Matt Hardin is in charge of the investigation. Hardin, as you may or may not know, made national headlines in Colorado Springs, Colorado before moving to Missouri a year ago with his family. He single handedly took down Shaun Phelps, known as the gutter of the west. He was rumored to have killed more people than smallpox. Please be careful if you are traveling at night or going anywhere that you are not sure if is safe.

On a lighter note, whew, just call me Mrs. Debbie Downer won't you, the Girl Scouts of America have added an additional cookie season for the fall. Records have shown that cookies and other treats are common gifts given during the holidays -"

Isaac only caught the end of the Girl Scout story as he walked back into the room smiling and thinking about thin mints in the fall. Traci leaned out of the shower asking, "Honey, what was that news story about?"

Isaac dropped his boxers and took a quick sip of his coffee. "Well, I have good news, Traci. They are going to start selling Girl Scout cookies twice a year. We will have them in the fall it looks like."

"Oh great because it is so easy to keep weight off during the holidays, why not throw a little cookie crystal meth into the equation."

Isaac pulled back the shower curtain and saw what he thought was a body made by the gods. "Honey, if this is you thinking you aren't a perfect ten then I don't know what will be."

She turned around, giving him a wet kiss. "Well, just remember I'm going to need to be fitting into a wedding dress at some point, and I'd like the size to be in the lower spectrum of the numbers one through ten."

Isaac stepped into the shower, giving her a hug. "Well, you'd better enjoy it while you can because eventually you are going to be huge with a million of my babies in your belly."

She rubbed him up and down until he shivered saying, "Oh it's too bad I'm marrying an old fart that isn't ready to go again right away."

He took the bait, and they practiced how they would be making those Hunter babies in the future. When they were done, he took his coffee back to the kitchen for a refill and a cup for Traci. His phone pinged and he looked down, seeing the flashing green light and hoping….no praying, that it wasn't work calling him on a Saturday.

Isaac swiped the phone to bring the droid's screen to life. A picture of Traci and him on the beach from that previous summer stared back at him, and he saw it was just a Facebook messenger staring back at him.

He set the phone back down, and it sounded like a video game going off within a matter of a minute. He knew that he shouldn't, but he picked the phone back up and opened the message and read a chain of messages from his buddy, Jack.

Jack - Hey what are you doing
Jack - Hey what's up today
Jack - Dickhead quit ignoring me
Jack - I can do this shit all day mo fo

Jack - Hey once you are done masturbating give me a call

Jack - Wow no one takes this long

Jack - Are you alive?

Jack - I'm alive, what are you wearing

Isaac - You have no life

Jack - Your girlfriend introduced me to my wife ass hat I had a life

Isaac - Yes and now you have Katy, boo fucking hoo

Jack - What are we implying

Isaac - That she married out of her league

Jack - I know I'm a catch

Isaac - No NO NO she could have done way fucking better, I mean she must have hit her fucking head at some point. Or you smoked her stupid is my only other thought

Jack - You touch my heart, come over and hold me

Isaac - Going on road trip, hold yourself

Jack - Where you going

Isaac - It doesn't matter, you aren't coming

Jack - You realize I'm already putting shoes on and will grab the wife

Isaac - I am going to kill you if you show up

Isaac - Jack?

Isaac - Hey?

Isaac - Don't do it

Isaac - Seriously it's a single day for us you aren't invited

Isaac - Don't come

Isaac walked back to the bedroom, his face flushed.

"You okay, Isaac? Did you burn your mouth on the coffee?"

"Not exactly. I think that we should leave, like now.

I'll throw these coffees into a couple to go cups, and we'll be outta here in ten."

"I'm not ready, food isn't packed, and we don't have a blanket to fool around on later. You are going to have to be patient. I swear anytime I make the faintest joke about a blow job you can't think about anything else until then."

"That isn't it....well that isn't completely it, honey."

"What did you do?"

"I didn't do anything. I picked up my phone because it sounded like it was going to explode."

"Did your work call you? I swear if you answered your work phone on a holiday you deserve what you get."

"Ouch honey, no it wasn't work. It was worse."

"Jack?"

"Correct. I told him we were going on a little road trip just the two of us."

"So the two of them are on their way here uninvited, aren't they?"

"Affirmative. If we leave before they get here it isn't going to be rude, right?"

She ran to the kitchen throwing everything into the picnic basket they would need and then rushed to the bedroom and grabbed an outfit for the day. She stared back at him standing there in awe drinking his coffee.

"Well, get your ass moving, or you aren't going to have to worry about sex of any sort again today. Once Katy sees this rock on my hand we aren't getting rid of her. She knows that she'll be my maid of honor. She's a planner and she'll start making lists the minute she sees it," she yelled.

Isaac, who hadn't even considered who'd be invited to the wedding let alone who he was going to have stand up with him, nodded slowly thinking of that car ride and shuddered. He raced through his closet throwing on jeans and a shirt, and the couple rushed out the door and down the three flights of stairs.

They ran outside laughing all the way, until they made it to Isaac's Impala when they stopped abruptly. Jack was sitting on the car's trunk and had his legs wrapped around Katy kissing her on the neck as she was trying to get away snorting and laughing from him nuzzling her neck. She said, "Oh for god sakes, Jack, Williams would you please let me go. We aren't teenagers for god sakes."

"Thank god for that, I hate rubbers."

"You think about one thing and one thing only, you realize that right?"

"Would you love me if I didn't?"

"I'd get sleep at night, at the very least."

Isaac said, "Thanks, Jack, for listening to me when I said, do not come, this is a private day for the two of us."

"I put my phone down the second you invited me, Isaac. I must have missed it. I am so sorry."

"I didn't invite you d-bag."

Katy slapped Jack on the chest saying, "You ass, I knew we weren't invited or we would've had a call from Traci. Traci, I am so sorry. I should've known better. I think the idea of a day with you and..."

Jack snapped in front of Katy's face startling her out of her gaze. She punched him in the arm yelling, "Oh my god that is so fucking rude. Traci....Oh my god would you look at the size of that thing. Oh my god, how did you not call me? When did it happen? How did it happen? Where did it happen?"

Jack tried to restrain himself, but it only lasted a second before he grabbed Isaac, yelling, "Oh my god! Tell me how she proposed to you? Did she do it this morning?"

Isaac started laughing trying to fight it back. Kate looked dead center at Jack. "Do you want that thing between your legs to only be for urinating purposes going forward for the foreseeable future? Sorry, Traci, he's a sexy man with the mind of a ten-year-old. I want to know everything, but you guys go ahead and have your day. It's fine. I can't wait to talk to your mom. She must be so excited!"

Traci said, "She doesn't actually know yet. We were keeping it a secret just for the day. Can you keep your mouth shut if I leave you for the day?"

"I could like totally say yes, but I'd kind of want you to know what you are going to come home to once you get back. I mean your mom is going to be pissed. I don't want to do that to you, but it's kind of out of my hands. Maids of honors have special privileges so yeah I'm sorry there isn't much that I can do to keep from spilling the beans. I'm actually already seeing myself visually typing out the message to about thirty to forty people that are going to need to know this."

Traci smiled nervously knowing the hell that would be unleashed if the words didn't come out of her mouth first to her mother and father. She whispered into Isaac's ear. "You realize that we have to kidnap them and take them with right?"

"But can we leave Jack there? Maybe a pack of wolves will adopt him.....or eat him. It's a win win either way, because he'll be gone."

"No I need him to help me pay the mortgage. He's going to buy all our groceries today to make up for crashing your engagement day."

Traci asked, "Groceries?"

Katy pointed to their miniature cooler and said, "No way that whatever you have in there is going to be enough for all four of us. If you wouldn't mind letting us borrow your cooler for the day we'll pack it full of sandwiches and beer and make a day out of it."

Isaac said, "Well if Jack gets punished by paying for all the food then hell, why don't we make this an overnight affair? We have a tent, really no reason why we couldn't all fit in there; it has three rooms and plenty of space."

"Is it the room with the moon roof in it, baby?" Traci asked.

Isaac picked her up, squeezed her tight thinking how much he enjoyed the engaged side of a relationship. "You know that it is, Traci."

The girls looked at each other and sprinted up the stairs to get extra clothes for all of them, and the men went to get the lantern, cooler, and tent from the back of the garage unit. "Dude, you really think that you've been together long enough to take the leap of all leaps?" Jack asked while they walked.

"Would I have bought her the engagement ring if I didn't think I could handle it? You know I've been in love with her longer than she has been single to date. Yeah, I am ready."

Jack laughed remembering their courting history. "Ahh, that is right. The vagina chronicles of you being single and she wasn't, but you insisted that there was no way that she was going to date that douchebag Aaron for very much longer. You were hell bent that you would wait and when she was single she would see just how great of a guy that you were. How many months did that go on for, super stud?"

"It doesn't matter now, does it Jack? Because I got the girl, and she loves me now, not him."

"Oh she doesn't love you, she would kill for you. You are all she talks about any time that she comes over and drinks wine with us."

"You obviously mean when she comes over to see Katy. Yeah I'm okay that she likes to talk about me, it means she isn't bored of me just yet."

"You know Katy comes to your guys' place quite often. I can't imagine how often she talks about me."

"Oh she does, but I think that it's more in the therapeutic sense, like Jack is such an asshole, I can't believe all the stupid shit that he does, I wish that his cock was at least four inches long, I think they have pills for-"

Jack punched him in the shoulder. "She has no complaints in that department asshat. Now where is your tent at so we can get on the road? This day trip just turned into a few day party. I hope that we can get enough beer to fit into this cooler you have."

Isaac pushed past, him rubbing his arm, and said, "The cooler is right there. See if you can reach it man."

Jack got up on tip toe and when he did used the back of his hand for payback to slap his friend, in the groin just as he was pulling down the oversized cooler, which would just barely fit in Isaac's sport utility. Jack instantly dropped his hands to his groin trying to stand in a way which didn't want to make him be sick, and in doing so dropped the cooler, which came down colliding with his head and sent him down to the ground. Isaac burst into laughter.

"You know I'm only laughing because I love you, brother."

Jack's face was turning red. "You know I kind of think that you would laugh regardless of whether or not you knew someone who just had that happen to them."

Isaac gave him a hand up, making sure to protect his mid-section and below. The two had everything they needed and within a few minutes were carrying everything back out to the street and began loading up the back of the sport utility.

*****

Traci and Katy went back up the three flights of stairs. Traci unlocked the door and when they got into the privacy of the apartment, Katy shut the door behind her and screamed at the top of her lungs sending a bolt of adrenaline through Traci. She rushed to Traci, squeezed her as tight as she could, and yelled, "You are going to get fucking married. Oh my god! This is the best thing that has happened in a very, very long time. I swear it feels like yesterday that Jack asked me, and I called and gave you the news. I can't believe Isaac finally pulled the trigger and asked you. This is so great."

"We've barely been dating for two years. Jesus I know people who date for almost a decade and haven't been asked."

"Those people are never ever going to be asked,

sweetheart. But really, who gives a shit about them? I can't believe this, I mean it. Is he excited too?"

"Well, I think that you might be more excited than the two of us put together, but that is only because….you are weird."

Katy walked to the kitchen, then went through cupboards knowing it was somewhere. When she was on the verge of giving up, she opened the freezer and saw a frosty clear bottle of vodka sitting in there.

"Now, I know that it is almost nine in the morning, but if we were having mimosas it'd be no less frowned upon." She grabbed two shot glasses and filled them to the brim. "Here is to my favorite girl ever. I love you so much, and I can't wait for your wedding. I'm sure Jack will be excited as well…..or at least about the party."

"You mean the open bar is what he will be excited about, and maybe the food."

"The only men excited about a wedding are dating men and the girlfriends who are imagining themselves in that dress and can't get that thought out of their heads when they get home."

"Yeah I've been there a time or two myself. I have a feeling that with the lingerie I'll pick up for our honeymoon and wedding night that Isaac will have plenty of things to be excited about as well."

"You got your engagement ring, now you need to glue yourself to his side. Those bitches stare at a married man thinking that shit is a challenge, like maybe I should steal this one because I already know that he believes in commitment, and if I can wrap my skinny slutty legs around him he'll be mine forever and would never ever cheat on me."

Traci patted her shoulder, sniffing the odorless frozen vodka. They did a quick clink of glasses, and then slammed them back. Traci licked her lips. "You, uh, think about that much there, sweetheart?"

"I hate just about every single girl, even the teenagers. They don't even know what they are doing, but they are the worst."

Traci poured off two more. "Only because I think you need it. Remember, we get groceries, and it's the four of us out there for the weekend. Peace and tranquility and our men all to ourselves with no schedule."

Chapter 5

Saturday

Traci was halfway done with a quick overnight bag with enough clothes for the four of them. A blaring horn sounded across the complex with someone holding it down hard. She thought that it was Isaac letting her know they were ready, and she was taking too long. She was thinking, sure, because it's a good thing to rush off into an overnight stay without making sure that you have everything you need.

She walked to the window and looked down at Isaac and Jack, who was trying to sneak in a quick smoke before his wife came down. Neither of the two were near the horn on the sport utility. They were both looking confused at the Mustang that had just pulled up. Traci could hear her dad saying how only an idiot, with too much money would take a perfectly good looking car and turn it into a piece of shit with all the add ons. This would go into a five-minute spiel about when he was younger and his older brother Ricky, who they had lost in the war, had a Mustang and back then they didn't add shit to the cars, no way. They stripped them down almost bare, making them look as close to racing stock cars as they could.

She craned her neck further, mouthing oh fuck when she saw who was in the car. All she could see was dark hair but by how the passenger was dressed, she could only assume who it was. Brandi let off the horn and rolled down the window.

"Uh, can I help you with something?" Isaac asked.

Brandi got out with a small family of beer bottles falling from the passenger side and clinking on the street. She saw Isaac, and a new smile found her face as she stumbled forward, letting him catch her. She said, "Oh my, aren't we a sweet piece of something. You can help me; I am looking for my best friend on the earth. Wait, no, on the planet!"

Jack exhaled a chain of smoke, ditching the butt in the storm drain. "Same thing, honey."

Brandi held up a finger hushing him. "Look, I am looking for my friend, Traci. I work with her, and I wanted to show her this boy that I found last night. I don't think she understands how good being single is. There is something wrong with her sometimes I think. She has an ass that could get all the boys. Oh, if she could go out with me, we'd never pay for drinks again."

Isaac knew immediately who the woman was and cringed. "You aren't looking for Traci Pendergrast are you? I mean it's another Traci that you are out looking for?"

"How many fucking hot ass women named Traci live here? Yes, I am looking for Traci Pendergrast. What is this fifty shades of fucking questions?" That brought on a barrage of laughter from only her. "What, you two don't have a sense of humor? Oh my god, oh my god, are you guys gay? Were you getting ready to go down to like the farmer's market to get fresh bread and flowers?"

Jack shook his head dramatically letting the loose hair frame his face. He walked up and put an arm around Isaac. Isaac rolled his eyes shaking his head wishing he had not answered his phone, and blaming no one but himself for it....and Jack, always Jack.

"No, no we aren't together, not like that, anyway I mean. My girlfriend is Traci Miller, and she's upstairs packing right now for a little road trip."

Brandi said, "Oh my god, you are Isaac. Ohhhhh she loves you. She talks about you all the time, always saying how it's bad to be out being a whore."

Jack, long married, said, "Wait, she calls you a whore?"

"No. She says something stupid like I shouldn't be so promiscuous or something like that. Makes her sound all smart and shit, but you know who's never hurting for pleasure?"

Jack smiled knowing the force of wives was quickly sending a message to his wife Katy upstairs. From experience, Jack knew she would be down here any second. He was aware how she felt about women, especially types like her and thought they were going to get along famously.

Jack said, "So why did you stop again? We are getting ready to head out any minute, believe it or not."

Brandi looked in the back of the sport utility. "You guys going out on a little trip are you?"

Isaac said, "Yeah we thought we'd go on a couple's camping trip for a day and what not."

"How many seats does this thing have? How many people can that tent hold?"

Isaac said, "Eight in the tent, six in the sport utility. Why?"

Brandi smiled, turning around and pounding on the hood of the Mustang to signal the guy to get out. He was out of the car in seconds looking at the hood.

"Christ, what the fuck is your problem? Those rings

cause scratches."

"Well, then maybe you shouldn't have been sitting in the fucking car in the first place. Who doesn't open a woman's car door, Travis!"

"Tony."

"What!"

"My name is Tony, not Travis; you must have me confused with someone else."

Brandi back peddled, not wanting to spend the weekend listening to him give her shit. She put on the puppy eyes and lips walking forward on her high heels making sure she could put as much shake in her step as possible without falling over. She gripped him in a tight hug rubbing herself against his front hard.

"Oh baby, don't be like that, you know I know your name."

Her hands disappeared for a moment in the front of his pants. By the look on the man's face, Isaac and Jack could tell that he did not give a shit if she called him Luther for the rest of the weekend if it meant that she'd continue doing that. He leaned in to kiss her back.

"Oh, I'm just giving you a hard time, baby, you know that. Don't get mad, Brandi."

She kissed his nose, patted his chest. "Good. Now I want you to meet Isaac and John."

"Jack, my name's Jack. Sorry, there's nothing you are allowed to do with your hands for me to deal with you calling me John."

Tony held out his hand. "What's up guys? You going on a trip or something?"

Isaac nodded wearily, hoping this wasn't going to go

to shit on them. "Yeah, you know, just kind of a spur of the moment thing. We are leaving just as soon as the ladies come downstairs."

Brandi said, "Oh that is just great, we'd love to go. Honey go get our overnight bags out of the car would you."

Jack said, "You are already packed; did Traci call you and invite you?"

"No need to silly boy, you guys just invited us. Oh this is going to be fun, nice day like today I'd love to get some color on this skin. I can't tell you how long it has been since I've been camping."

Isaac just stared at Jack, unsure what to say. They watched in horror as Tony walked to the back of his trunk and pulled out two bags that they could only assume were used for hook up nights. Isaac said, "Sorry if you misunderstood me but-"

Traci yelled from the doorway trying to hold a mess of items and keeping a foot up to hold the door for Katy. "Brandi, what the hell are you doing up so early on a Saturday? What are you doing here?"

Brandi said, "Who's up early? I haven't made it to bed yet. I tell you, he might not look like much but Tony....I mean Tony here can fuck like a damn jackrabbit. I might be in love."

Brandi was ignorant to the fact that she was screaming across the courtyard to the apartments and more than one window slammed shut after the small introduction of who Tony was.

Traci said, "Right, and that is great, nothing like a good all night fucking, but that doesn't actually answer what you are doing here. Do you need something? It isn't work is it? I have a three-day awesome weekend that is even better now since I am going to get the opportunity to spend the weekend with my best friend and my fiancé in the great wild wilderness."

Brandi said, "And don't forget about your best work friend. While you two were upstairs your boyfriend here invited us to come with."

Traci nodded slowly, looking at Tony still dressed in party gear from the previous night. "By us you mean your new acquaintance over there?"

"Oh we've been fuck buddies for at least a month now. It's not easy finding someone that doesn't want a relationship but can really nail you to the bed, if you know what I mean."

Kate stepped in holding a hand out. "Hi, I'm Katy. It's too bad there isn't enough room for you to go. You see that tent just isn't big enough for three couples, besides I'm sure you and your jack rabbit over there are going to have better things to do than go on a camping trip right?"

Brandi could sense the hostility and said, "Well, Jack and Isaac practically begged us to come. We already have our stuff in the back of your truck. We really just need some beer and food for the weekend and we are kind of set to go. I don't know about you, but I can't wait to get to know all of you better. You just seem so damn sweet."

Katy through clenched teeth said, "Oh watch out or I'll give you a fucking cavity."

Traci walked over putting the rest of the items in the sport utility leaning in close whispering, "What the hell were you thinking, baby? I can't believe you invited them. You don't really like strangers all that much, are you feeling okay?"

"I was feeling just fine until your psycho friend showed up and invited herself along. You know I wanted you all to myself. Hell, I would get rid of Jack if I could."

Brandi leaned in and said, "How about instead of whispering we get this show on the road. So where are we going anyway?"

"We are headed to the state park, shouldn't be more than four hours from here. It's way out in the middle of nowhere. Just a farmhouse here and there between," Isaac said regrettably.

"Well, sounds like we aren't only going to need beer, there's a strong chance that strong alcohol is going to be a necessity. I think we are gonna cat nap on the way there if you don't mind?"

Isaac, Katy, and Traci simultaneously answered 'no' all at one time. Brandi said, "Well, doesn't that just make me feel all warm and fuzzy." She checked her pockets, which didn't exist, and looked to Tony. "Tony, honey, do you think that you could."

He didn't say anything. He already knew he'd save time and be able to catch the sleep that he'd been thinking about. Tony looked through his bills handing Isaac a small handful of twenties. "We can get you some change, shit this will pay for the entire weekend," Isaac said after seeing the stack Tony had given him.

"Don't worry about it. I had a pretty tame week, there's plenty more where that came from."

They climbed into the SUV and before they made it a mile, Brandi and Tony were curled in the backseat snoring lightly. Within a half hour they were on the open road and had a truck full of supplies to get them through the next few days.

Katy leaned up in between the front seats and said, "So, they are fun aren't they? What the hell are we going to do with the two of them?"

"They are harmless. I work with her, I can't say I know much of anything about him though. She always just made it sound like she's all about being single."

"How did she miss the rock on your hand?"

"Brandi, really, and I mean *really,* doesn't give a shit about that kind of thing. Like it doesn't matter to her if you are married or not. She probably looks more down upon people if they are than not. Monogamous isn't really like her favorite word."

"Soooo she's pretty much a slut?"

"She has a good heart? I don't know, yes, she does not have a lot of down nights. I'm not sticking up for her, it's just how she is. You can ask her yourself, and she'll give you a graphic description above all else, but at least she isn't fake. I'm sure she'll be a hell of a girl to party with, just watch your husband. You shouldn't have too many troubles with lover boy back there."

Isaac looked in the rearview and whispered, "If he drools on my fucking seats he's dead, I'm just saying. Actually for that matter, neither of them better get any bodily fluids in my truck of any type."

"Dad, are we almost there yet? I'm bored. I want a snack. I have to go pee," Jack said, already bored with the drive.

Katy went back to him, wrapping her arms around him. "Oh, honey, are we not letting you in on the conversation? We were just saying that she's going to be a lot of fun to party with. You just make sure that if she starts doing a strip tease dance under extreme intoxication that you remember if you look I'm going to probably let you know what feeling like a virgin feels like all over again."

Jack looked at her blankly. "You realize that it isn't my fault right? I mean there could be a five-hundred-pound woman doing a jiggle dance, and we'd still feel compelled to look. It's a gene running through our body. It isn't my fault. Isaac, you know what I mean don't you?"

"Don't bring me into this. If she gets wild I'm taking a walk with my fiancé here, and that is all there is to it. You do what you need to. Good luck with that jiggle show; sounds like you will be a one hand man for a while if you piss the old lady off."

Katy slapped Isaac's shoulder. "I'm sorry, who are you calling old lady?"

Isaac said, "Well, I can remember more than one night someone being the one telling us at three in the morning that we should head to the strip club so that we can keep drinking."

"Well, that's just art, and besides that was before we got married, and about fifteen pounds ago when I looked as good as them."

Jack tilted her face to him and gave her a long kiss, running his hands down to her rear end. "Oh Katy, I love the pounds that you put on. There isn't anything wrong with there being just a little extra behind you. I hate to see you go, but I love to watch you leave."

Katy unclicked her belt climbing over and straddling him, and the two of them shared a few kisses. They only broke when Tony started ripping farts in his sleep, coincidentally interrupting Brandi's sleep as she had her head in his lap. She pushed up, sniffing, and Katy, who was the only one with a good view, started laughing uncontrollably. Brandi found a new position out of the danger zone and went back to sleep.

"Well, aren't we just mature," Jack said with no lack of disgust.

Katy said, "Oh god it hurts just a little. That is great! I mean, he smells like ass and it's kind of burning my nose, but it was momentarily funny."

Isaac let the windows down a few inches. "Let's get some of that funny out of the car holy shit."

"Oh you remember those all night benders buddy, nobody's body can handle that shit. Just remember his liver is used to this, those two are probably going to be able to drink the four of us under the table," Jack replied.

"I don't know, I think we will be able to last....until at least eleven," his wife countered.

"Just make sure you don't get so drunk that you pass out on me. We wouldn't want to miss a nice star filled night." He searched through his pocket, wanting to take a pic of the two of them and realized he didn't have his phone. "Can I use your phone Katy? I wanted to get a picture of the two of us."

She looked through her purse. "Sorry, fuck I can't believe I forgot my damn phone. What if there is an emergency?"

"We have our phones, don't worry about it," Isaac said.

Isaac, pulled his out showing them, and when he hit

the camera to come up said, "Doesn't really look like it matters we don't have any service anyways. We'll be fine."

"And if we have an emergency?" Katy asked.

"What, do you want to wait for an ambulance to get all the way out there or would you rather get in the truck and meet them halfway? Besides, all we plan on doing is hiking and drinking, we'll be fine. Back in our parents' day people used to leave town for days on end without being able to reach the outside world. Don't worry, I promise I'll send you all the photos from the weekend so you can post them on Facebook."

Traci smiled, looking at her phone as well; at the moment she didn't care that it wasn't anything more than an expensive camera. She knew she should have at least checked in with her mom and dad but knew they were in nowheresville, and there wouldn't be any opportunity of doing it now. The sign for the park came up and an outage sign was hanging on it. "You have got to be fucking kidding me. What the fuck?" Isaac said.

"Anger management, honey. Let's see what it says," Traci said.

"It says that it's fucking closed. What the hell? Why didn't they have that on their webpage? They need to update that shit."

Katy walked out looking at the sign seeing they were doing maintenance on the dam and didn't want people staying there. The sign advised the work was scheduled to begin within the next week. She looked around smiling and walked over to the roped gate dropping it down and said, "Oops."

Isaac smiled, pulling through. She reattached the

rope letting others know not to enter. They drove through slowly and Jack joked, "You realize how many movies have started this way. I mean the only thing we are missing is a black kid."

"Yeah but we have a pretty rich boy, and a slut so we are pretty fucking close aren't we?" Isaac said laughing.

"Oh would you two shut up. You are going to bring bad karma to us."

Katy climbed back in and asked, "Shut up about what?"

"My fiancé here and your significant not-getting-laid other are talking about this is how a scary movie starts."

Katy nodded and said, "That's right, you guys should know, especially you, Jack. She is not a fan of anything scary. Happy is good and safe and keeps her from peeing her pants."

"That was once, ass, and The Hills Have Eyes is some seriously creepy shit. You can't tell me that doesn't fuck with you. My friend who loves scary movies watched that while she was pregnant, and she was done with scary movies after that. I mean she was die hard horror and gore and that movie put that shit to sleep," Traci said.

"Are you going to be able to still enjoy yourself out here?" Jack asked.

Katy watched as the trees' canopy engulfed them, putting them into a momentary darkness. "Well, shit, it's what, one o'clock? I think we can have lunch, and then we are going to have to begin drinking early. Do you think the sleeping beauties back there are going to be able to wake up long enough to help us get everything set up?" She asked looking at Brandi and Tony.

"Do you really want to wake them up? It's like a baby, you get them up and they aren't going back to sleep for like ninety hours or however long babies stay up for. Seems like they are awake all the time, though," Jack replied.

"Jack and I can knock it out, we are pros, don't worry about it. If you get too many guys going at once on something, you are going to over complicate it. If you lovely ladies want to get lunch ready, we will rock out on the tent and stuff."

"Geez Isaac, I don't know if we are going to be able to put those pre-made sandwiches on plates and then add chips and dip. Traci isn't much of a cook, definitely not an old married woman yet, so I'll have to teach her the ways of cooking."

"Well, remember the most important thing is going to be making sure that my beer does not, I repeat does not, get empty," Jack told Katy with a humorous glint in his eyes.

Katy gave him a kiss. "Just remember you don't want to fall asleep before me, or you aren't going to be able to enjoy the great outdoors, baby."

"Oh, I'll nap today if I need to, don't you worry about it."

"Yeah you know my dad naps, it's something old guys do I've heard. You guys make sure you get him a can of prune juice too, keep the old man regular."

Jack leaned forward. "You realize I'm only like three years older than you, don't you?"

"Yeah, it's a shame to think what can happen in that short amount of time. Probably need Viagra and depends. Do your farts drip now?"

"Oh my god, if anyone gives this horn-ball a single pill of Viagra I will kill myself, I'm not kidding," Katy said. "You'd think after this many years he'd settle down but no, he is still a thirty-year-old with a fifteen-year-old teenager's penis."

"Yeah probably the same size to," Isaac said, not able to stop himself said.

Jack hit his belt release and leaned forward to give Isaac a shoulder hit that he would not soon forget and Isaac thought about punching the brakes hard and letting the rear end of the truck slide, but looked at the two sleeping in the back and used his willpower to stop himself.

Traci said, "Holy shit that just made my life. This place is beautiful. Second best thing today besides the engagement hands down."

Isaac cleared his throat, rubbing her leg up high, and she said, "Okay fifth best thing, because wow did we celebrate the engagement like there was no tomorrow."

Traci squealed excitedly and pointed to one of the many, many open spots. "We need to take that spot. Look at that, there is a place for a fire and a clearing next to the lake. That couldn't be any more perfect, could it?"

Jack said, "No, not unless it was a five-star hotel in the Caribbean, but who are we kidding? I deem this spot thou spot to get shit faced for the next few days."

Isaac pulled in, and they got the truck unpacked leaving Tony and Brandi sleeping in their spots. They were walking on eggshells, happy to let them sleep if they wanted to. Isaac and Jack were both confident, that if she was woken from her slumber prematurely she would be a royal bitch to deal with. They got the tent set up in no time and to their credit were able to consume two beers each during that time.

Brandi came out of the truck, leaving Tony sleeping and looked around trying to take in the view. She saw the lake and stumbled over in her high heels, doing her best to not break her neck. She found a clear spot to sit down thew off the heels and let her feet soak. She pulled out a smoke and lay back flat, looking up at the blue sky and the crisp white clouds passing overhead lazily. A stream of smoke poured out from around the cigarette clenched between her teeth. The smoke swirled into the air disappearing into nothing. Katy was filling plates with chips and sandwiches. She said, "Not that we really need the help, but it's lovely she decided that she didn't need to help with lunch."

Traci said, "She's not so much a morning person. Given it's afternoon but I'd be confident that it's about the same thing on the weekends to her. We might want to give her just a little bit to wake up. She can make up her own plate when she's ready. Boys are you ready to eat?"

Jack nodded. "Yeah, you guys want to take the plates down by the lake?"

They all nodded to this and within five minutes were sitting down by the lake watching the Canada geese floating lazily across the water in front of them with an equal number of adults to babies.

"Oh my god, this is the most beautiful place ever. This would have been a good spot to pop the question, Isaac."

Isaac smiled, thinking of how they had gone through and done the ritual and was just content as could be. "Nah, I'm good with how I did it. But yeah, this is picture perfect, huh?"

Traci pulled out her phone taking a picture of the two of them. She did not see the watcher across the lake. Jack said, "So only because I know that Katy is going to ask, let me beat her to it. How did you ask?"

Isaac smiled and got an elbow to the gut.

"It was actually in the morning today when we were still in bed. It was very romantic and perfect," Traci answered.

Jack could see the smile trying to break free on his best friend's face and shook his head. "Probably even climatic, huh?"

This earned him an elbow to his own gut. "Don't be crude and ruin something beautiful. God, men are so dumb."

Chapter 6

Saturday

Tony sat in the SUV's rear seat with his head facing directly up, snoring loudly. The stranger walked slowly around the truck, looking in the distance at the five other occupants of the campsite. He sat watching Tony's chest rise and fall, wanting badly to stop that from happening. He tapped on the glass and waited patiently. When Tony did not so much as stir in his sleep, he brought back a giant of a hand and slammed the window with his open palm shaking, both the window and the truck. Tony jumped in his seat, startled, and awake looking around wild-eyed and wiping the line of drool making its way down his chin.

"Jesus Christ!" Tony looked around, breathing heavy, fists clenched, but he saw no one. "Yeah, real fucking funny people. Why didn't you guys wake me when we got here, damn it?"

Tony was moving his lips and tongue around trying to gain some sort of saliva. He felt the all-night party he and Brandi pulled was now catching up to him. He looked around and saw the tent and the campsite already set up. A short moment of guilt for being uninvited in the first place and not helping with the work ran through his head. It only lasted a moment; there was the thought that no one woke him up, and he couldn't help it if he was sleeping. Tony took off his seatbelt, looking at the seat in front of him and trying to figure out how to get it to move so he could get out.

After a minute Tony gave up looking for the hidden

button or lever, and as gracefully as he could, threw a leg over the second seat and went over. He lost his balance and fell between the front and second seat's feet space. "Fucking Christ, stupid ass seats. If he had a fucking real car, this wouldn't be an issue. I don't need this stupid shit right after waking up, damn it."

Tony got up from the floor to his knees. A shadow fell across his face as he was pushing himself up, and he fell backwards. "Real fucking funny, assholes. Real fucking funny. Fuck with the new guy, yeah I get it. That fucking hurt man. I would have helped you with the tent if you would've woken my ass up."

Tony looked up, cocking his head to the side and mouthing what the fuck. "I left town to get a nut off and I end up out with a bunch of weirdos for the weekend, that's great. Hey lose the mask man, you are creeping me out and we don't know each other all that well."

The figure slowly shook his head no and blew hot air on the outside of the window creating a small circle of condensation. He drew an unhappy face on the fogged window and stood back. Tony, not wanting to look weak, slipped out of the sport utility, puffed up his chest, and looked down and saw whoever it was was not standing on a bucket like he'd thought.

"Jack?" The stranger shook his no. "Isaac?" No again. "I didn't know we had anyone else meeting us out here."

The stranger brought a machete from behind his back. Tony jumped away but slammed into the door. He raised an arm to protect himself, and the stranger brought the machete down, slashing across his forearm and cutting him from wrist to elbow. Tony screamed in agony, but his yells fell upon deaf ears that cared little about his pain. "What the fuck is wrong with you?"

The stranger knelt down and gripped Tony's arm which was bleeding like a stuck pig. He extended his index finger still holding the machete and stuck a finger up through the cut into his knuckle and drew a face but this time it was a happy one.

Tony kicked at the man's feet, but it did little to keep him from doing what he wanted to. The man gripped Tony's hair pulling him forward and slamming his head against the back of the truck and smearing the face he'd drawn, leaving nothing but a bloody smudge.

Tony tried to get up despite being dazed and the man gripped his machete again rising back up to his feet. When Tony looked up at him with tears in his eyes the man's arm moved without hesitation. The blade whistled in the air as it split the front of his neck into two clean pieces leaving a flap of skin. Tony tried to talk but the gash across his throat left him without the ability to speak. Tony gripped his neck in an effort to try and stop the bleeding. Fresh crimson blood poured through between his fingers. He tried to speak but only bloody air bubbles came from his mouth. The man knelt back down, staring into Tony's eyes, watching the tears run freely from them.

The man stood gripping the machete and turned to walk back out of sight. Tony sat there watching as his world began to turn black. He saw the edge of the trees hundreds of yards away and knew there was no chance in hell he would be able to make it there before he bled out. The thought of how long it would take to get back to the hospital ran through his mind. He was angry now for falling asleep in the back of the truck. The fact he was clueless as to how far away he was from any type of medical clinic horrified him.

Tony staggered as he got up from the grass and made his way sloppily around the side of the truck, leaving blood stains the entire way beneath him and on the white truck. He looked around wild-eyed trying to see where the stranger had disappeared. He feared for the others coming back, but the thought of his own demise was more important at this moment than their safety. He opened the car door, hit the horn, and did not let up.

Chapter 7

Saturday

The four sitting together heard it at the same time. They listened for a moment, waiting for it to stop.

"Dude, I'm pretty sure that is your car man. I hope pretty boy isn't fucking up your ride," Jack said.

"Why, would he be doing that?"

"I don't know. Why would he be honking your horn out in the middle of nowhere? You think maybe he's lonely?"

"Maybe he doesn't like waking up by himself in some stranger's car in the middle of nowhere by himself," Traci said.

When the horn did not stop, Isaac got up from his lunch. "Fucking idiot. Okay, I guess I'll go check on him and see what the hell he wants."

"Don't worry about it we'll all go." Katy said, adding. "Besides, we are done eating anyways."

"Would it be too much to ask you guys to bring me and Traci a few beers back with you?"

"I'm sorry, but I'm not staying out in the woods with you, Jack. I came out here to spend the weekend with the man I love, not sitting around waiting for more beer with his best friend."

"Oh, that hurts. Come on, Traci."

The four all went walking to the edge of the woods and back to the clearing. Isaac thought he saw something out of the corner of his eye in the distance by the road, but a belligerent screaming came from his left. He looked over to see Brandi, fists clenched, screaming.

"Shut up Tony! I'm coming god damn it, there's no reason to be such a dick. You were sleeping anyway you asshole! Shut up, shut up, shut up!"

The four stared at her baffled. The amount of noise this tiny, thin woman could produce was mind numbing and ear splitting as well. "Jesus Christ, what is wrong with her?" Isaac asked.

"I don't know brother, maybe she didn't get quite as long of a cat nap as she needed?" Jack replied

Brandi marched, high heels in hand with a purpose, one filled with hate. The other four made their way but did not go nearly as quickly as her. The idea of having to talk to her when she was this mad did not make any of them want to catch up to her. When she got within twenty yards of the camp, she hurled her high heels one after another.

"Why don't we give them a few minutes to talk? Maybe he just wants her and only her," Isaac reasoned. "It's only going to make shit more awkward if we go there and they don't want us to be a part of their talk."

They watched as she disappeared around the side of the truck and when she did, Brandi screamed even louder than before. This wasn't a scream of anger, nor one to let them know she was going to rip his head off. This scream was because she was scared for his life and had no clue what to do. She backed up, hunched over dry heaving, and yelled.

"Somebody fucking help me. Somebody help him. Please now, come here!"

The four sprinted, and as they rounded the sport utility's rear end, they saw the red covered grass. Brandi was down on the ground reaching towards Tony like a disease and didn't want to touch him. She could only see blood and didn't know what to do with the wounds. Jack pushed her out of the way. When she fell, she saw her blood soaked legs and started screaming all over again. Jack took his shirt off and pressed it to Tony's wound, holding it as tight as possible without choking the man. Jack made an assumption.

"Why the fuck did you do this to yourself?"

"What are you talking about? How do you know?" Katy asked.

Jack pointed with his free hand at his arm. "Look at this cut. There is no stitching this easily; he's going to need hours to fix this. He wanted to commit suicide. Look at this. Brandi was he acting weird last night?"

Brandi just stared back, tears pouring now and a mess of makeup running down her cheeks.

"I don't know. We drank, we fucked, that's what we do, so no, I guess he was normal. I didn't even know he had a knife on him that could do that."

"Well, it sure as hell seems like he did."

Isaac pulled the rear door open and put the seats down, making it possible for them to lay Tony flat in the sport utility. "He doesn't have time for this talking. We need to get out of here and do it now. I need someone to sit in the back with him and apply pressure. Jack, I don't think you are gonna fit with him in there. Traci, can you handle it honey?"

"Well, I'm sure as hell not going to make any promises, but I'll do my damnedest to do my best."

Jack pointed with his free hand. "Now look here, you

put pressure across the front of his neck, and you hold this around his arm. Isaac, we lift on three. You ready?"

Isaac knelt down and the two lifted on three sliding Tony into the rear of the SUV. He started to shake, and his eyes opened looking around insanely trying to speak.

"I don't know what you were thinking, but it wasn't the answer! We are taking you to the hospital. We are going to get you help," Traci screamed.

Jack shut the door once she was situated. Isaac slid behind the wheel.

"I don't know when we'll be back, but you guys wait here. Try to clean Brandi up and give her some of the good stuff. I think she could use it."

Isaac slid in, started the vehicle, and accelerated while not flooring it, and sped down the gravel road. He watched as they made it one, two, three hundred yards away and then a half-mile and then out of seeing distance. He kept his foot steady on the gas and the vehicle in the middle of the gravel road. He'd been on enough of them growing up with his dad to know that if you got on the side of the road, it would suck you in and send you straight into the ditch.

He looked into the mirror seeing a bloody engagement ring on his fiancé's hand and tried to think of something to lighten the moment, but little seemed appropriate. He turned around saying, "Hey, you doing okay back there, baby? You are doing so good. He's going to thank you one day for helping to save him, I promise."

Isaac only saw it for a moment, and in that brief second was unsure if he really did see it, or if his eyes were playing tricks on him. "Oh fuck, hold on."

He veered the truck to the side trying to miss the giant man in the white mask. When he did, he over corrected too quickly never letting off of the gas pedal. This was his first of many mistakes. He felt the back end of the SUV giving way and sliding wildly left and right. He yelled, "Hold on to something, baby, it's gonna be-"

The truck's entire left side went up into the air and began a number of rolls. Traci and Tony were thrown violently up and down and back and forth on the inside. They looked more like a racquetball on a wild ride then two humans. Tony's wounds having no pressure to keep them closed reopened and began spraying everything and everyone in the car as a geyser of blood began when the SUV made its first of many rolls.

When the SUV came to a rest the front end was sticking out of the ditch, and it was now dead. Isaac tried to push up off the seat, but everything available to his senses hurt. He lifted his head and felt the spins instantly take place. The radiator busted, and again, he couldn't tell if his eyes were playing tricks on him. He watched what looked like a man with a white mask walking towards him before he blacked out.

Chapter 8

Traci's parents' home Sunday

Chuck sat in his seat flipping through channels. His wife Rosa sat watching him and shaking her head. He saw her judging eyes.

"What woman? What am I possibly doing wrong watching a damn show?"

"Because you and I both know perfectly well what we are going to watch. I would rather watch a hundred other shows, even no shows at all, but we know what you're going to watch so just go to the damn channel."

"You know NASCAR doesn't start till noon. I'm sure as hell not going to watch those little prissy asshole announcers talk for two hours."

She looked at the time. "Well, then you need to find something to do because that roast won't be done until noon, and I'm not watching channel flicking for the next two hours, Chuck Pendergrast! You do know that there is a cable guide channel you can go to and magically see what is on every channel we have and it will even take you there once you've finally made up your mind."

"Aren't you a damn comedian? One hundred channels, and there ain't shit on, you know how many channels they had when I was a kid?"

"You mean they had television back then. I just thought you watched the horses walking around on dirt roads."

"Oh you are a regular riot this morning, sweetheart."

"Well, I'm just stating the obvious. Why don't you

just do what we both know you are going to do and find the oldest show that you can, that no one wants to watch, and put that on. I'm sure you can find Dirty Dozen.....Oh wait, let's watch Easy Rider, or The Hustler, for the millionth time."

"The Hustler, thank you very much, is a god damned good movie. You know what I think I have that on Blu-ray. They had that damn thing for like three bucks at Wal-Mart, only a fool would've passed up on that one."

Rosa pinched the bridge of her nose trying to think to herself why she didn't just put old batteries in the remote and he'd sit there too lazy to get up.

"Just find something to watch, dear, before we hurt each other."

"Don't worry, I'm going to go for a drive. Maybe I'll see if Traci and dipshit want to come over for lunch. We got enough, right?"

"Don't call Isaac that. He is a wonderful young man and you know it. Don't be angry with him because she spends more time with him now than us."

"I'm not jealous of him. Are you kidding me? She'll always be my little baby."

"Well, you never know, pretty soon maybe they'll settle down and have some of their-"

He held up a hand signaling her to stop. Chuck didn't care how old Traci was or how beautiful she was as she matured into a woman, he still only saw a messy faced six year old with pigtails looking up at him smiling. He sighed thinking what they would have to do to have grandkids and wanted to stab his eyes out trying not to think of that son of a bitch and what he would do to his daughter.

"God damn it woman, you know not to talk about that shit with me. It screws me up all day long. She was supposed to wait till she was thirty five or forty to even date."

"You realize we were eighteen when we married, just before you left for basic training. Is there a reason you want her to wait to be an old woman before getting married?"

"Yeah, real fucking simple one, too. I want to be dead and gone so I don't have to think about her sleeping with someone. It gets my damn stomach going like a son of a bitch."

"Well, just try not to keel over too soon, I'm pretty sure if there's anyone in this entire world besides myself that she wants at her wedding it would have to be you."

He smiled, pushing up out of his chair and tossing the remote to his wife. "You know what, it's a hell of a lot harder to tell me no to my face than to one of those stupid little texts you guys do. I'm going for a drive; I'll be back by lunch."

Rosa laughed. "Are you going to their apartment, Chuck?"

"I can't say for sure. I'm just going for a drive, besides I'm sure the race will be shit, and I'm about out of smokes. Last thing I need to do is run out mid race and have to deal with that stress nicotine free."

"Yeah, you'd better get two packs honey, as cheap as they are. And good for you. I really wouldn't want you to run out, dear."

"Nobody appreciates a smartass, Rosa. Especially after kidding around about his only daughter. If i happen to end up over there I'll make sure and let them know there is plenty of food to eat."

"You make sure you knock, and don't just go walking in unannounced."

"It's ten o'clock in the morning for god sakes; I expect them to be awake and ready for the day."

"Just remember I warned you dear. You might open a-"

"Yeah, yeah, I know. Well if you hear any gunshot reports on the news it's probably just me finding out that kids their age don't have a reason to get up and moving in the morning. Horrible for Isaac though."

"You be good, Chuck. Jesus you need a hobby besides worrying about your baby. Maybe you could get a job at Wal-Mart greeting people. Or maybe we could get a Fitbit and start going for walks?"

"I don't need one of them stupid Fitbit to tell me I don't do shit. I can save a couple hundred bucks and tell you myself. Now I'll be back, you make sure that gravy is thick and the bread warm. I'll see you later."

"You make sure you are back before the roast is done. I need you to cut it for me and to drop the fried bread down in the grease. Unless you want a nice side of cauliflower with it?"

Chuck did not answer. He knew there wasn't any in the house, and until he was dead and buried the only vegetable she would serve him would be corn on the cob with a side of butter and salt. Chuck stepped on the running board and got in to his Silverado. He revved the engine and pulled out slowly, nodding and giving one finger salutes until he was off his block and away from those who knew him. He did not hate the fact that Traci only lived a few minutes from their place. He liked to think the fact that it was extremely reasonably priced was not the reason the two lovebirds had taken it. He was much more content telling himself it was because they were so close.

He had no intentions of going anywhere and pulled out a carton of smokes from beneath his seat grabbing two packs. He pulled up and looked at her apartment not seeing the windows open. He couldn't figure it was cold enough in there to keep the windows closed. He worked his way up the steps, wondering why in the hell anyone would pick a floor this high up. When he made it, he knocked twice then tried the door handle wanting to keep them on their feet. Never safe. Never alone. Dad can always be around the corner so don't touch my fucking daughter, were the exact thoughts that raced through his mind.

After a few minutes, no one answered, and he began pounding his fist on the door. Within another minute neighbors were slowly starting to look outside to see what was going on. Chuck turned around, not unfriendly or shy in the least, and pointed to their door.

"Hey, any of you all know where these two went? I'm her dad, and I want to invite her over for roast today."

Chuck got nothing in return but blank faces and nodded his head. "Okay, well thanks for the help amigos."

He pulled out his cell phone and dialing his daughter heard nothing on the inside. He felt his pants for the extra key on the ring and went in. What he saw on the inside didn't make him feel all that much better. It looked like the place had been ransacked. He saw a pair of past due notices on the table and looked through them. The first was for their cell phone bill, and there were a few under that which he didn't pay any attention to.

"Well, that's fucking great. Hard to get a phone call kids when you ain't got any service on your damn phone. Of course kids knowing everything nowadays, probably never gave it so much as a second thought to pay their damn bills on time."

Chuck pulled out his wallet tossing it on the table and opened the phone bill paying both of theirs. When he went to hang up the lady with an English accent said, "Remember as this is a holiday it will be up to seventy-two hours before the phone will be reactivated and available."

Chuck called Rosa. "Now tell me that I shouldn't be nervous, or paranoid will ya?"

"You are always paranoid Chuck; it isn't really a wonderful quality either. You make me nervous half the time when there isn't anything to be worried about. Let me guess, you ended up over at Traci's place didn't you? Were you able to talk them into lunch?"

"Well, believe it or not I wasn't able to talk them into anything, because neither of them were here. I don't know where the hell they are and I don't know how to get ahold of them because dipshit, or Mr. Wonderful Isaac, didn't pay their damn cell phone bills. I can't reach them and don't know how to handle it. The neighbors haven't seen them either. I looked outside and saw her car sitting there and Katy's little car sitting outside as well. I'm wondering if they tried to go out for the weekend. I don't like not knowing what is going on. Do you think we should call the police?"

"Why, because your twenty-something daughter hasn't checked in with you? Is there any cause for concern that you are going to be able to tell them about?"

"You mean other than the fucking killer out on the loose, and them probably being ignorant to it all? No, other than that, there isn't anything that we should be concerned about. Did I mention the killer on the loose out killing people for absolutely no reason at all? The one with the knife that leaves people completely mutilated and fucked up?"

"Chuck, are you insane? What are you trying to do, give me a heart attack? You can't tell someone something like that. For good god, call your friend at the force and get someone finding out where in the hell they are immediately. At the least hopefully you will be able to secure a missing person's report on the two of them."

"I'm not calling about Mr. Wonderful. I'm calling about my baby."

"Well, Mr. Wonderful doesn't have anyone to inquire about him with the exception of our daughter, who is missing at the moment."

"I'll be more than happy to make mention to Nick about it, it'd be my pleasure."

"You call me back the minute you talk to someone, Chuck. Try to keep yourself calm. Last thing you need to do is have a stroke up on the third floor. I can imagine that you are in her apartment by now?"

"Yep, and I'm even drinking one of their beers for the damn trouble. Parents shouldn't have to worry about ignorant shit like this. Kids are supposed to check in and let us know what is going on."

"Yes, it's absolutely amazing at their age that they want to have a life of their own."

"Goodbye, dear."

Chuck looked at his phone trying to figure out the web browser on it and gave up. He searched through the cupboards until he found a small phonebook with an inch of dust on it. He did his best not to disturb the dust and looked up the police's phone number. He called, asking for his high school buddy, Nick. They'd enlisted together and they had gone through the marines together and were better than brothers because they were fellow marines. Someone stuck with the weekend shift answered less than interested in the call.

"Washbaun County Police, how may I direct your call?"

"Good morning, I need to speak to Chief Lambert, please. Tell him it's Chuck calling."

"Just Chuck?"

"Chuck, is that too difficult for you to understand, son?"

"No, sir. I understand right fine, but he isn't here. He's off today. It's Sunday, so he's probably getting ready to watch the race on television. You know about the race right?"

"Christ, it's Missouri, of course I know about the race. So, he isn't there. I'll call him at home."

"Well, sir he doesn't like to be bugged at home on"

"I tell you what, you pull his ass out of the jungle in Vietnam and he's more than damn happy to take a phone call from you any given day of the week."

When the man didn't respond Chuck hit the end button yelling, "What a dipshit," as he hung up the phone. He knew Nick's number by heart and wasted no time calling it. His wife Tricia answered on the fourth ring.

"Chief Lambert's residence, how may I help ya?"

"Hey, Tricia, it's Chuck. I can't find Traci anywhere. She isn't answering her phone, but that's just because her dipshit boyfriend didn't pay the bill. I know Rosa sent a text yesterday to check on her, and she said that she hasn't posted anything on Facebook either."

Tricia handed the phone to Nick saying, "Oh, hey Chuck. Nick, Traci is MIA."

Lambert took the phone smiling and shaking his head. "Sounds like a serious missing person case, Chuck."

"Don't fuck with me, Lambert; you know I don't worry about shit that I don't need to worry about. Is there anything you can do? Don't make me talk to Tricia again."

"Damn it, Pendergrast, the boys and the grandkids were going to come over this afternoon. You are going to make me miss seeing the kids. I even had some racing hats for them to wear during the race today."

"Boo fucking hoo. You don't think that I want to be home? I had a very busy day ahead of me also, I'll have you know."

"Rosa making roast and gravy. God, that woman can make a great roast and the gravy-"

"Focus, Lambert. Jesus man, we need to get moving on this. Her boyfriend wasn't here either. He drives a Kia Sorrento, and his license plates are Washbaun County, as well, and the number is Echo Foxtrot Golf 562. He is supposed to have LoJack on that thing. I would think if you guys just make a call to the company that they could find it."

"Okay I got it written down. You go on home; I'll call

the guy that does missing persons. He's working those cases on missing people that have been in the news lately as well. I hope that she doesn't need found, but he's going to be pissed if he has to waste an entire day off out looking for a twenty-something and her boyfriend."

"If that is the case I'll buy the kid a top shelf liquor bottle. You can't pass up an offer like that."

"You can when the guy doesn't drink. Why don't you figure out some other way to bribe an officer of the law later? If I know him he's still working at home."

"You'll keep me informed then, right, Nick?"

"Yeah, I will keep you up to date."

"Thanks."

Chapter 9

Sunday

Tricia gave Nick a hug from behind holding a bottle of wine out in front of him in one hand with a corkscrew in the other hand swinging them teasingly in front of him. She had been married to the chief long enough to know when he was going to have to go to work.

"For god sakes Nicky, can't you ever tell someone no?"

"Honey, it's Chuck. What do you expect me to say? I owe him a lifetime of favors and besides, if it was Josh or Jake missing wouldn't you want me to move Heaven and Earth to find them? I don't even know if there is an issue but with that fucking crazy man running around I don't want to take any chances with anyone. Throw in there that it is Traci, someone that we've had over here since she was in diapers, and I think you can see my point, right?"

Tricia laid her head down on his shoulder, pouting and nodding her head yes. "So do you think that we can drink this later tonight after we've found her and had a good laugh at whatever stupid story they have to come up with?"

"You know how Chuck is about his girl. He wouldn't let anything happen to her. If he could keep her in a bubble, he'd be perfectly content in life. I'm pretty sure that he hates the fact that she is out on her own and on top of all that living with her boyfriend."

"Not much he can do about it legally at this point is there? You get your cute butt moving and have it back here by supper, or this bottle of wine is all mine. I don't want you to miss this pie either, you know the grandkids will not show mercy when it is time to eat."

"And Grandma Lambert can't say no to them and save her loving, hardworking husband a slice?"

"Not when little Lisa shows me those eyes. They are as blue as the sky; I swear she was sent from the heavens just for me."

"She's only cute when she leaves my pie alone. Now you save me a piece or I promise you, woman, I'm going to make sure I get nothing but Barefoot all week on the way home to drink. You let me know how that sounds to you?"

"Okay fine, but if she puts out the pouty lip when I tell her there are no seconds I'm happily throwing you under the bus, Mr. Lambert."

Nick slid on his sidearm and grabbed his keys to the work car. "Well, for god sakes everyone has limits. If she shows you the pouty lip, you give her the damn pie. You can bake me a fresh one on Monday."

"That isn't how it works, Nick. You be careful out there."

"Honey, you realize that it doesn't do much good to tell me that, right? I always try to come home to you. Besides, I'll probably be sitting on my ass in the break room watching the race and waiting to hear back from Detective Hardin with details. The way that man works there is a good chance that he is going to be done before I even make myself comfortable down there."

"I'm allowed to worry. If I didn't you better make sure I didn't up your life insurance to a nice seven-figure payout."

"You know me, honey; I'm not worth shit dead."

"Like I said, I can worry if I want to, even if you aren't worth anything."

He leaned in gripping her tight and bowing her down giving her a quick wet kiss and brought her back up making sure she was steady before heading out the front door.

She went to the pie, cut a healthy piece, wrapped it, and placed it in the microwave far out of the reach of Lisa who would need a step stool to get close to reaching it. She shook her head, looking at a picture of Nick and the two grandkids sitting on his lap by their lake house. *You better know how much I love you, you damn fool.*

Chapter 10

Sunday

Detective Matt Hardin sat at the kitchen table skimming over reports and shaking his head. His wife Jamie came up from behind and gave him a hug and kissed him on top of the head.

"Honey, you think you might turn it off for a little bit of the day while there is still some daylight left out there?"

"Turn what off, Jamie?"

"You know exactly what I mean. You turn off the job, you put your papers in the briefcase, and you put it and all these horrible images away for the day. You know there is more to life than work, right?"

"I know, but-"

"But nothing. It isn't your fault that so many-"

He slammed his hands on the table making it and everything on it bounce to the floor.

"You don't seem to realize anything, Jamie. It might not be my fault, and it might not be solely up to me to find these fuckers, but you forget one thing. Once the first dead body shows up and it's assigned to me, I have to look every single parent in the eyes and tell them to their face that their loved ones aren't coming home. I have to be the bearer of bad news, and you don't want to see the death in their eyes, the heartbreak that is happening. The longer I take doing what I want on the weekends, the time I waste in the yard, playing with the kids, taking you guys out to dinner, is the same time that piece of devil's spawn has to plan out what he's going to do next. I love you, I love the kids, and you all know that, but this isn't the kind of job where you can just let shit go. You have got to understand that it's a ticking time bomb."

Jamie's lip quivered a bit. She knew he had a temper but didn't want to deal with it on a Sunday. "I'm sorry, Matt. I wasn't trying to upset you. You are right though and it's selfish of me to ask you to leave it alone when I know how important it is to you."

Matt lifted her head. "Honey, it isn't important to me. It's important to the mothers and fathers of the dead. They want to see justice. They want this piece of shit brought down. If it wasn't something I was so goddamned good at I would quit and find another job. I am just waiting for this one to make that one mistake. That one thing when they make it is what counts, and I have to be ready and on top of my game."

She patted his chest. "Well, then, let's hope that it happens quickly for your sake and ours. I don't think you can handle too much more of this living. It isn't easy on any of us. You know I have always been proud of your work, but when the shit starts getting this close to home we need to reconsider where home is."

"Meaning what?"

"That when you find them, you are going to start looking into other job openings in places where the killers don't do their work."

"Don't go down that road again."

"I'm down it, and I'm looking. There are plenty of security jobs out there that are private and safe that you are going to interview for. I think you would be a natural for any of them. You need to start thinking about your old age.

You aren't going to be able to chase crazies down for your entire life; at some point, you are going to need to slow down. You are almost forty, Matt. I'm just saying start thinking about it before it's too late."

Matt stomped to the fridge to grab a cold beer and almost ripped off the top of the bottle as he pulled the cap from it. He drank half of it, trying to catch his train of thought before responding to his wife again.

"You know what, this is something that we can talk about at a later date and time. I love you, I love the kids, and I'll try to take a break a little bit later. We can grill up some burgers if you get the meat laid out?"

The phone began to ring on his belt, and he ripped it off forgetting it was his work phone and he was still worked up from the talk with his wife. "Who is it, damn it?"

"Detective Hardin?" Nick asked. "Its Chief Lambert. Is everything alright, son?"

"Just fucking peachy. Just don't tell me that you are calling about another dead body?"

"No, this time I'm calling about a live one."

"You don't have someone else that you can give a call to, Chief?"

"Yeah, I have an entire department under me, Hardin, but I'm choosing to call you. Were you ever in the service, son?"

"I don't understand how that is relevant."

"Well, an answer like that screams no to me. The reason it's relevant, as you put it so eloquently, is the person who we presume to be alive is the daughter of my best friend. The same best friend who enlisted in the marines with me over thirty years ago and pulled my ass through a few miles worth of shit you wouldn't want to visit in your worse nightmares during Vietnam."

"Gotcha. It's a debt you owe him, so you want to give him everything you have. What are the details?"

"There are two people actually, but he's pretty sure we'll find the two of them together. His daughter's phone isn't working. He saw a past due notice on the table and all calls go straight to voicemail. The two missing are, the boyfriend, an Isaac Hunter, and Traci Pendergrast, and she's twenty-seven. Her dad said that they have LoJack on his sport utility. It's a Kia Sorrento, white, and it could be as simple as that."

"So I'm trying to find a young couple in love, chief? You realize how awkward that's going to be if I have to break something up like a romantic getaway, right?"

"Son, if I cared I wouldn't be asking you to do it. He's worried, and from time to time it's going to be a good thing if you have a few favors that you've done for people. He sent me a few recent photos of the two in question that he found on her Facebook page you can use for a reference. I'll forward them over to you. Echo Foxtrot Golf 562 is the license plate on his SUV. I assume you are going to start there with the LoJack?"

"Yeah, if he has it then that sure as hell would speed up the process. You sit tight, I'll report back when I got something. Is there anything else I need to know, sir?"

"Yeah, there's one pretty important detail. This man is a brother to me. His daughter is my daughter. I love that kid like she is my own. You get her in, and I'll make sure that you have everything you need, and then some, if there's something you need for your main case. I mean I don't know what else you could use or what you are missing, but I'm sure there is always something isn't there?"

"Yeah, usually. I'll get on it, Chief. I have kids so I understand the importance fully."

By the time he was done his wife had already packed his briefcase and taken his beer, replacing it with an ice cold Pepsi.

"I gotta go. I promise I wasn't expecting this."

"We never do, Matt. Give what I said some thought, but, honey, do one thing for me?"

"What's that?"

"You go find that man's daughter."

Matt pulled her in, giving her a kiss on the forehead, he walked through the house seeing his kids in the living room watching Disney as he left, not a care in the world.

Chapter 11

Sunday -Three hours later

Matt drove down the highway following the GPS signal in his car. He looked around for the mile marker as he called the chief.

"This is Detective Hardin. I am following the coordinates given to me. It shows that there is a state park here and it is closed. I'm going to go in. I can call you back and let you-"

"Detective, I've been sitting here for three hours waiting and doing absolutely nothing useful. You set the phone down, you mute it, but you don't hang up on me. I know how sick my friend is by now. I am going to keep him up to date with news as I get it. Last thing I want is him running off halfcocked looking for her."

"Agreed, I need to go take off the chain to pull in. I'll be back with you in a few minutes."

Matt sat the phone down and opened the gate but, unlike the group the previous day, did not replace it back where it belonged. He drove slowly and when he pulled up, saw the SUV crashed and on its top and grabbed the phone.

"Chief, I found the Sorrento, but I don't have any good news yet. It is upside down and half in the ditch. I'm going to go check it out now.

Chapter 12

Saturday

Isaac woke to the sounds of screaming. Not just any screaming, but Traci's screams. They filled the SUV, bringing him back awake. He lifted his head up, feeling the spins still there, and sat back down. He tried to push up realizing he still had his seatbelt on and clicked it off.

"Traci, baby are you okay?"

He looked at his rearview mirror that was hanging now with only a shard of glass still attached. He saw her pushed up against his side of the truck kicking wildly. His vision was still blurry, and when it came into full focus, a fuck me minute hit him like a hammer.

"Get this fucker away, god damn it!" Traci screamed at the top of her lungs.

Isaac turned in his seat and saw what looked like a hook, the type you might pick bales of hay up with. But instead of doing its normal job this one was going after his fiancé. He watched as the hook dug down deep into flesh, fresh blood came spurting out and sprayed across the man's arm and covered his hand in new warm blood.

"Fuck!"

Traci screamed again. "He's got Tony. He has Tony!"

The hook started to disappear from view as Tony began to slide out of the truck feet first. He wasn't able to scream, but there were unmistakable tears starting and painting a small path through his dirty and bloody cheeks down the side of his face. Isaac rolled over to the back kicking at the man's hand. His efforts were too little and too late, all the force he had to hold on to Tony might as well have been from a child because before he knew it Tony was gone. Isaac ducked down and saw the man dragging Tony into the middle of the road. He climbed back into the front seat wanting to know what was wrong with this man. He noticed he hadn't been daydreaming and his eyes hadn't been playing tricks on him either.

"Oh my god."

"What, what is he doing to Tony, Isaac?"

"You don't want to look, I promise."

Traci pushed herself up screaming at the pain erupting in her ankle. "Isaac, I think it's my ankle. I don't know for sure, but it might be broken or sprained."

"Can you walk on it?"

"I'm in the back of your truck, I have no idea. I guarantee if it means you and me getting away you won't have to help me."

Isaac was going to say something else when the man brought machete down. He stared watching, everything he had seen in movies was not like real life. He had one hand gripping a handful of Tony's hair. With the other, he chopped at his neck over and over again, the bone, the fat, the muscle, everything he could until he had gotten Tony's head removed from his body. When he was done, he held up the head for Isaac to see, looking more than a little proud of himself.

Traci, who had been trying to get herself free from the back and over to him to get out of the truck said, "What, what did he do to Tony?"

"A lot. We need to get the fuck out of here. I mean now. If you think you can run, then do it, but if not you say something and I'll throw your ass over my shoulder and be gone with you. Do you have your phone in your pocket?"

"Yep it's in there; I can feel it."

"That's good. I want you to call the police. Better yet, call 911 and let them know there's a fucking psychopath on the loose and we-"

"Yeah I get it. Shut up and get us out of here!"

Isaac looked around in the truck, thinking how everything including hatchets were now sitting at the camp. "There isn't shit. I don't have so much as a stick to throw at that guy!"

Traci hit 911 on the phone and hit send. An automated voice came answered.

"Thank you for trying to make your call. The owner of this phone is behind or decided to no longer use Sunrise Phone Services. If you think you've reached this message in-"

"Isaac, when is the last time you paid the cell phone bills?"

"I thought we had it on auto pay?"

"Oh my God, we are going to die because of something this stupid. I cannot believe this, god fucking damn it!"

"No one said anything about dying. We just can't call for help."

"In case you didn't notice, Isaac, that guy just chopped of Tony's head, and he looks like he's playing with his mouth right now. He has a machete as long as my leg, and he seems to know how to use it."

Isaac did not respond. He knew they were limited on time, and they needed to get the hell out of there. He tried to open the door as quietly as he could, but when Isaac tried to push it open the door stayed shut. He ran his arm around the side of the door, feeling the dents along its side, and knew it had been jammed shut. He looked into the back of the truck and rolled over the top of the seat. He slid out pulling Traci behind him. When she tried to walk on her leg she screamed.

The stranger looked up when he heard her cries, tilting his head to the side.

"We have to go. We need to get out of here and back to the others. I don't know what else to do, Isaac."

Isaac thought of where they were and in comparison to the road, and knew there were little options. They would stand a better chance at getting out of this alive with Jack to help him. The man stood between the two of them and the road back to their campsite. When Traci screamed again he started walking with purpose toward the two of them with a head dripping blood in one hand, and the bloody machete in the other.

"We need to get into the woods. We are going to have to go the long way around, there isn't any choice about it. We aren't going to get around him safely, not with you banged up. I still don't know how I'm doing, but we can worry about that later."

"What if you pass out? What am I supposed to do then?"

"You hobble like you never have before and make it back to Jack. You tell him to put the machete or the axe that I brought into that guy's head."

The two of them made their way down the ditch and back up the other side, heading through a field to try and elude the man following them. He was silent, and that made things all the creepier for them. Isaac held firmly to Traci letting her use him as a crutch. He prayed they could make it back to Jack before anything else bad happened today.

Chapter 13

Sunday

"Chief, I think you better call in some boys on their day off today. We are going to need them."

"Oh my god, what, what do you see?"

"A crime scene, sir. The SUV is all kinds of banged up. There's a man that I am hoping isn't Isaac."

"Why, is he hurt? Why don't you give me some fucking information here?"

"Is he hurt? Yes, he is hurt. His head was chopped off. I don't see the head anywhere; someone might have taken it as a trophy. This screams of the killer though. It is a brutal scene. I am going to get out and look, but you need to get someone besides me out here. We are going to need a search team, and the quicker we can do this the faster we can put it to bed and know what is going on."

The chief sat back in his chair, taking a deep breath. He'd met the kid a dozen times but for the life of him couldn't think of one distinguishing mark he had on his body or tattoo he could remember.

"Initial thoughts?" Lambert asked.

"There's a trail of blood heading back deeper into the campground. My guess is that someone is carrying their trophy, and it's dripping as they are walking. There is blood all over the inside of his truck. There isn't anyone else in there, but this place is bloody. It looks to be a day old from the dried blood. Whatever happened is in the past by now."

The Chief covered the phone's receiver and screamed. "Bynum, DeBryan, Nulty get in here now."

When his yell fell on ears that were too busy watching the race, he gripped the first thing he could sending it toward the wall, shattering what turned out to be his coffee cup.

"I said, Get the fuck in here, and do it now!"

The three appeared at the door looking around wildly. Nulty tried to smile but it looked more like he needed to have a movement.

"Everything okay in here, Chief Lambert?"

Bynum choked on a laugh. "Yeah, he's always throwing coffee cups on a Sunday."

DeBryan had the most tenure and knew damn well to keep his mouth shut. The chief had seen some serious shit in his days and freaking out wasn't something he typically did. "Last lap of the race. Sorry, chief. Sorry about that."

The chief nodded. "I want you to call the next county over and tell them we need a chopper and all available resources that they can offer. Hardin just called. He's a few hours away and called saying there is a decapitated white male in a state park, one that is closed currently, along with a crashed SUV and enough blood to paint a house with."

Nulty ran off immediately to call and get them a ride.

"So do you think it's him again?" Bynum asked.

Lambert nodded slowly yes and then no thinking about it, and said, "Well, for their sakes I pray that it isn't."

"Sorry sir, is there something else that we need to know here?"

"One of the people that more than likely was in the SUV was my goddaughter. The only reason Hardin found that so quick was because he can do magical things with LoJack and has connections from previous departments he's worked at. They know the jobs that he is usually assigned to so he can skip through some of the bullshit political tape and just get locations."

"Sir, are you sure you want to go with on this? It isn't going to be too personal, is it?" DeBryan asked.

The chief stood, pulling out his drawer and stared down at his Glock. He pulled it out checking that, yes, there was a bullet in the chamber. He attached it to his belt, and to accompany that got his handcuffs and extra mags to clip on his left hip.

"It doesn't matter if it's too personal. If she's still out there, she's been there at least a day from what it sounds like and has got to be horrified at what is going on. I pray that if the killer was out there that she got away from him."

He heard Hardin's words again. *You definitely need to get out here, Chief.*

"What? What else?"

"There is a camp ground I assume belongs to them. It's been torn all to hell. I don't see anyone here so I'm going to head back to the gates to meet everyone from the other counties."

* * * * *

The helicopter landed on the highway. They'd radioed saying they were going to drop in on the campground and Hardin had asked if they were fucking stupid. Finding the people, he told them, was as important as anything but the fact there was evidence here, evidence in his mind he could hopefully use to one day track down the killer, was as important, he told them, as finding the people. He knew the MO of the man who was doing this by now. The fact they still had hopes of finding these kids alive was something that made him question how much these people had a grasp on reality. By the time he made it to the edge of the park there were three other squad cars sitting there waiting for him.

Hardin formally greeted everyone, rushing through the pleasantries. One of the local county police put down a map on the hood, and they started looking at entry and exit points. The officers showed him this was the only way in and out. The entire thing circled around and ended up sending you back right here. They showed him there were some farm houses here and there, but for the most part it was trees for as far as the eye could see with trails created over time by hikers and off road bikers, etc.

When the helicopter landed, they divided up into the cars and started their ride to the horror show. They passed slowly by Isaac's SUV, and Hardin pointed it out to Lambert, who was riding shotgun with two of the deputies in back.

"If you look, it appears that he flipped the truck. There is damage that runs the top and both sides. It's obvious that he ended up in the ditch, and I'll save you the visual for yourself of seeing it but the inside of that is coated in dried blood. Whatever happened obviously wasn't from the crash, it was a third party who had nothing but bad intentions. I'd assume even, that he or she was the reason that they went off the roadside."

Nulty leaned forward from the back seat laughing. "Wait, you think that the killer could be a woman?"

"We don't find these people," Hardin said, "until days after they have been dead and gone. Now couple that with the fact that it took multiple machete strikes on that young man's neck to chop his head off, and it would lead me to believe that every option needs to be explored."

"Yeah but chicks aren't serial killers. You probably know that by now, right?" Bynum asked.

"Yeah you're right, what do I know? Have you ever heard of Elizabeth Bathory? They called her the Blood Countess. She lived around 1585."

"No, of course not, why should I? Wait, let me guess, she killed a man?"

"No, Bynum. She was more into the ladies....well teenage peasants. She alone made this killer look like a pussy. As accurate as the numbers could be back then, she killed and tortured around 650 girls. A little more in this century was The Giggling Nanny who killed four out of five of her ex-husbands, her mom, sister, and grandson."

The three men stared at Hardin who never broke eye contact with the road.

"Hey, are you shitting us? The Giggling Nanny?" Lambert asked.

"Yeah, she would laugh during interrogations. She was a real peach. Look up there, that's the campsite."

"Hey, so it's just those two cases?" Nulty asked.

"No those are just two that I thought of, I could list off another eight without thinking. If we assume that it's a man, then we ignore every single detail being presented to us if it says that it is a woman. If you don't look at every option then you won't know what you are looking for until it's too late. You find a woman that acts like a victim thinking it can't be the killer and then bam." He slammed his hands on the steering wheel, startling the three passengers with him. "And that is it and you are gone. She pulls out a gun and blows off the back of your head, or slices your throat open, or about a hundred painful ways I can think of to die."

Lambert looked out the window, thinking he'd been happy to trade anyone else here for a seat in their car. When they pulled up they saw the tent or what was left of it. There was only a third of it still standing. The men got out and started for the field. Hardin whistled to them; when they turned around he tossed a box of blue gloves to Bynum.

"Let's try not to fuck up my scene."

"Well, let's not forget this is still a missing person's case now." Lambert added.

"Just don't you guys forget, the longer we go the better the chance you aren't going to find anyone alive. If I were you, I'd see if there are any dogs we can have brought in. There's a chance we can get a scent for the girl. We want to find her either way though."

The two officers walked into the field, leaving Lambert and Hardin by the car. "You don't give me a lot of hope, Hardin, about finding this girl.....did I mention the missing is my goddaughter?"

"It doesn't matter if she is your daughter or wife Chief. I'm not going to scream about you finding her and how it's guaranteed. This killer has got a one hundred percent success rate. He or she goes for the kill and that is what happens. I'm sorry I am not being more optimistic but statistically it doesn't look good."

Chapter 14

Saturday

The three young people left at the campsite watched as the SUV disappeared, going over the hill and back down the other side. They were all shaken up. Jack and Brandi were both covered in blood and looked a mess. Katy placed an arm around Brandi.

"Come on, Brandi, we have some water back by the tent. Let's go back there and wait."

Brandi shook her off. Emotions she hadn't realized she had for Tony came pouring out and left her in a state of mind she did not know she was capable of.

"What the fuck are you talking about water? I need a drink, god damn it. What the fuck was he thinking? He didn't act weird the entire night last night. He was laughing and having a good time. He wasn't suicidal, that's for sure. And a man that had his brains fucked out had nothing to be upset about. He had a smile on his face more than once last night. What was he thinking? He has it made. He has everything anyone would ever want and then some."

"You know....I could probably use a drink too," Jack said.

Katy pointed to the two of them. "What I meant was that maybe you might want to wash the blood off of yourselves and get a change of clothes."

They looked at themselves., "Let's just go back to the water's edge. I think we are going to need some serious water to get all of this off. Can you grab some clothes for us? I'm sure something of you or Traci's is going to fit her

99

right?"

Katy assessed Brandi, nodding. "Nothing like loose clothes anyways right? You'll be fine Jack; the two of you wear identical summer attire anywhere, shorts and a shirt and you are good to go."

Jack shrugged, his attire at the moment was about the last thing running through his mind. "I just realized we don't have any way of contacting them and finding out what is going on."

"They'll come back. The news isn't going to change anything. They are going to be wrecked when they get back. It'd probably be good if we leave them some cold drinks."

Jack grabbed three beers, stuffing one into each pocket and one for the walk, and said, "There's plenty of booze and beer, besides I'm confident right now we are as mentally fucked up as anyone could be."

They walked down to the lake. Jack stripped off his shorts, the only thing left he'd had on after making a makeshift bandage on Tony's neck. He stepped into the cool water, running it over his chest, arms, and hands until the drying blood was washed away, revealing bronze tinted skin again. Brandi watched, and Katy kept a close eye on her. She felt a bit uncomfortable having her husband in nothing but a pair of tight, now very wet, sport boxers. Brandi slammed back some sort of concoction she'd mixed herself, ignoring the beer, saying how it was too many calories. Katy couldn't imagine how anyone could possibly be worried about your figure at a time like this, but only screamed on the inside at Brandi as she stripped down to her unmentionables in order to wash herself, as well. Jack dried and when they were both dressed in borrowed clothes they headed back to the campsite.

Jack went to the firewood Isaac and he had collected, not paying attention to it. He was focused on his wife and making sure she was really doing okay and not just saying she was. When his hand came back wet it caught his attention. He looked down and saw it was sticky and red. He moved his fingers around trying to think what it could be and very quickly had the answer, the one that he didn't want to be true. He fell backward dropping the firewood and choked on his own scream.

When Brandi and Katy saw the look on his face there was no question he'd seen a ghost

"Jack? Baby, what is it? What is wrong?"

He held up his bloody hand, pointing it at the woodpile. She saw it and misinterpreted what she saw.

"What's wrong with your hand? Did you cut yourself? Fuck this day!" Katy yelled.

Jack tried to speak, but nothing came out. He just mouthed the words woodpile, woodpile. Katy leaned in, watching his face. She'd never seen him go so pale so fast even at his worst condition. She dropped to her knees in front of him, and when she finally figured out what he was saying, she turned around to look at the wood. Tony's dead eyes were staring back at her. She screamed and there was no choking on her part there was just piercing noise. This grew in intensity when Brandi looked at the pile in her near buzzed state and began screaming as well.

Jack jumped up from the ground, somewhat in a daze. "If he didn't commit suicide then who...who did that to him?"

The stranger stepped out slowly and in no hurry. Jack

saw him and took a few steps back. The white mask was smeared with blood. Jack assumed it was Tony's, which freaked him out. The fact Tony's head was here and his best friends in the entire world took him to get medical care hit home. When it did it was hard enough that it made his stomach turn and he puked the beer out that he had been consuming as if he hated it. Jack gasped to catch his breath.

"Who.....who....who are you? Where are my friends? What the fuck is going on? Is this some sort of sick fucking joke?"

The man shook his head no. It was hard to stare directly at the man because of the afternoon sun peeking over his shoulder. The stranger shook his head slowly; he dragged a hand across the tent as he walked forward leaving blood streaks on it as he let his hand fall back to his side.

Jack looked down at the girls who were frozen in place, He yelled, "I need you girls to get your asses up and I need it right now! We need to leave, there's obviously something fucking wrong with this guy, and I'm not going to wait around to see what it is. We need to go and try to find Isaac and Traci. We need to see if they are okay and get out of here."

"What do you want from us?" Brandi asked the stranger.

The man pulled the machete from his belt, held it up with one hand, and with the other ran a bloodied finger around his heart and then pointed at them.

"What? Are you trying to say that you want our hearts?" Katy asked.

The man put a finger to his temple and then gave a

thumbs up sign. This infuriated Jack. He made sure Katy was completely on her feet.

"I love you baby, I want you two to run. You run like you've never had to in your life."

"Jack, baby, don't do anything stupid. We can run together. We don't need to do anything, we can just run!"

"He'll catch up to us. He's got a foot on us, it doesn't matter how far we go he's going to be able to keep up, and from the looks of him he's been out here for a while."

Brandi walked over slowly towards Katy. "If he wants to keep us alive, you might want to take him up on that. Now come on let's start running while the giant is still peaceful."

"He isn't your husband, you bitch. He doesn't fuck me because I'm just there; he loves my ass and I love him. I'm not going to leave him. It's both of us that make it or none of us; there is no middle ground on this one."

Jack, who was by far the laid-back one of the two, made no question about it. He screamed at the two of them leaving no choice but to listen to his words. He bent down, preparing to rush the giant of a man. Brandi reached for Katy's hand taking away her choice to stay or leave, and pulled her into the distance.

"I can see some smoke coming from over there, maybe someone else is out here camping. Someone with a fucking car, we can hope, or better yet a gun."

Katy fought at first, and to her surprise, a hand came from nowhere and Brandi slapped her open handed with a good amount of force sending a numbing feeling across Katy's face. Jack winced seeing that.

"She's right baby, you need to go with her. There

isn't anything you can do to help. The two of you standing on each other's shoulders you are barely as tall as him."

Katy thought about the fact the two girls' weight combined probably didn't come close to what the man in front of them was pushing. They took off at a run and the man turned his focus to Jack. Katy looked back over her shoulder as she was practically be dragged into the distance.

"I love you!" Jack screamed.

He bent down further, gripping one of the branches of wood, and the stranger held up the machete, putting a finger to the blade and running it across. The stranger held out a hand teasing Jack to come forward. Jack now wished the hatchet hadn't been put away with the other gear already. He looked at the branch, trying to think of what to do, and knew all options were shit. He rushed the man, taking a swing with the stick. The man brought the machete down and connected with the branch, not slicing through it but knocking it out of Jack's hand.

Jack backed up a few steps trying to keep his balance. He had no death wish, but knew if he could give the girls enough time to get a head start that at least they would have a chance at surviving. He ran at the man, again and brought up a foot to the man's groin. He closed his legs around Jack's making him fall off balance. When the man released his leg Jack tried to crab walk backwards. The man walked towards him, kicking his legs out. When Jack held up his hand, the man brought down the machete.

Chapter 15

Sunday

Bynum screamed to anyone who would listen, waving his arms wildly. Lambert held up a hand for him to wait a minute trying to think of what he would do if he had to tell his best friend that his daughter wasn't coming back. He thought of the look in Chuck's eyes and felt like someone was ripping his heart from his chest.

"Hey, Chief....just because the statistics say that she probably isn't alive, doesn't mean that she can't be. There's always that one miracle child that pulls through situations with no chance of living and they do. So don't lose all hope. I'm just not trying to fill you with it. That isn't my place to do so only to end up having the worse be found," Hardin said.

Lambert nodded, walking into the field. "Well, let's hope for her and her family's sake that we do find her and her boyfriend."

When they made it to Bynum, he used the gloved hand and looked a bit green in the face as he showed them a finger. Hardin looked and said, "Well, at least it isn't the woman's"

Bynum said, "How the hell do you know-"

Lambert cut him off. "You date a lot of girls with hairy knuckles and fingers?"

"Shit, what dates? This uniform doesn't do jack shit for me getting dates, sir."

Lambert thought about his wife and how they'd met over a speeding ticket. "Well, you are doing something wrong kid. You can figure that one out on your own. Look at the dark hair. It's a guy. I'd bet money on it. Besides, look at how low the fingernail is cut. No female is going to look like that."

"So now we have another factor to weigh in with. There's a second male involved in this," Hardin said.

"I don't understand," Nulty said.

"Try to keep up Nulty. You saw the victim by the truck, correct?"

"You know I did. So what?"

"Was he missing anything?"

"You mean besides everything from the neck up?"

"Yes, besides the stupidly obvious, Nulty."

"No, apparently not."

"Well, if you'd have noted everything about him then you would have seen that he didn't have any missing fingers. I'd say from the blood on scene here the finger wasn't dropped here and this was where it took place."

Lambert said, "Bag it, print it, and send it to get looked at and see if the person is in the system. Maybe he has some minor in his history that will have him in the system."

Hardin walked away from them looking around; he yelled, "Hey, Chief I think I got something bigger than a finger over here. You've seen this Isaac fellow right?"

"Yeah more than once, why?"

"Well, why don't you come over here and tell me if this head belongs to him?"

Lambert did the sign of the cross praying it wasn't, but not wanting to wish suffering on another family at the same time. When he walked around the side of the tent he saw a head staring back at him, and Tony's face gave him an instant relief. "Does that look like it'd fit on the corpse by the SUV, Hardin?"

Hardin knelt down looking at it moving it around to examine it. "Well, the removal of this head sure as hell would have been as brutal as the one by the crashed SUV."

Lambert was keeping track. "So, what we have is Isaac, Traci, and two males. Our list of people to find is growing."

Hardin said, "Well, three men and one girl screams to me that there's probably more girls. We just haven't found any of them. Or pieces of them, to say more accurately. Let's hope that the men tried to save them and they got away as a best case scenario."

Lambert said, "This shit's just getting worse."

"Yeah, imagine this as your day job."

"How the hell do you turn it off, Hardin?"

"I don't know. I guess I'll let you know once I figure out a way to turn it off at night. This shit goes home with you."

Hardin walked away leaving it at that and watching the blood as it disappeared into the grass heading towards the tree line.

"We need to follow this. I have a bad feeling we are going to find where they were hiding in the woods."

Chapter 16

Saturday

Jack screamed at the top of his lungs as he watched his finger fall to the grass below. Tears filled his eyes and streamed down his cheeks. He watched as the blood soaked his freshly cleaned arm, turning it red in the bright sunlight. When the man brought the machete up a second time, Jack turned to the side, trying to push the pain out of his thoughts if only for long enough to escape. He went the wrong way and rolled into the tent, knocking half of it over. Jack jumped to his feet avoiding the swing, and heard the blade whistling as it made its way toward him.

Jack looked over his shoulder as he ran trying to see where the girls ran to, not wanting to follow them, but he could not see them anywhere. The man did not wait for Jack to tire and began a run of his own. For some reason Jack was surprised that he was running. He always thought that like in the movies, the killers could out walk you no matter how fast you were attempting to run. "Leave us alone damn it!"

The man started to cut the lead Jack had on him, his giant frame was enough to slowly start to catch up. The stranger most definitely appeared to be a mad man at first sight. He had a machete clenched in one blood splattered hand and a piece of wood in the other. Just as Jack thought once he hit the inside of the tree line it would provide him some sort of safety, the man hurled the branch at him, striking him in the spine and knocking him to the ground.

Jack tried to push up but it was too late, the man was

already upon him. When he tried to push up from the ground the stranger put one monstrous foot on Jack's back and pushed him back down to the ground. When he tried a second time the stranger kicked him in the gut, bent down to pick up the heavy branch and struck Jack across the back of the head, twice. Jack started to watch as the world spun, and he could hear a familiar voice screaming his name and filled him with the smallest morsel of hope.

Chapter 17

Saturday

Isaac pulled Traci behind him. She was crying uncontrollably, and Isaac could not blame her in any way.

"Baby, when we get out of this, not if, we are going to go away somewhere tropical and safe and with a fuck ton of alcohol."

Traci laughed, wiping at her eyes as they made it into the clearing. She had fought him to take the road back to the camp but he had lobbied against it, telling her there was no way they wanted to run into that monster again. When they made it to where they could see the campsite they watched as Brandi and Katy were heading into the woods. Isaac looked back at the campsite and could see Jack being manhandled as he was trying to, what could only be assumed was an attempt to save the women's life, or at least give them a hell of a head start.

Isaac gripped Traci by both arms. "You need to stay in the tree line and follow the girls. I want you to try to catch up to them. Is your ankle going to be able to do that?"

"Yeah, I'm sure I'm able to, but why are you talking like you don't want to go with me? What in god's name do you think that you are going to do?"

"You can see Jack, right? You know that we can't just leave him out there; he's unarmed, and that twisted fuck is not going to chop off his damn head, I promise you that."

Traci held up her hand with her newly acquired engagement ring. "Sorry, but maybe you forgot that you are engaged to me. You need to go with me. It isn't possible to marry a dead man, you know that right?"

Isaac smiled, giving her a quick but deep kiss. "Look Traci, I'm pretty sure that Katy isn't going to want to be a widow at age twenty-seven. If there is anything that I can do to help him I need to do it. There isn't anyone else out here that is going to be able to do something if I don't."

"Why, do you have to be such a fool and so brave at the same time?"

"Just remember those are only a few of my enduring traits that you cherish about me, right?"

She put her head on his chest, taking a whiff of his cologne and deodorant, which was a masculine scent that helped her sleep at night. She thought about it being the last time that she would have the opportunity to get that smell and started to cry even harder. She started hitting his chest.

"You come back, damn it. You don't leave me. You don't die. Get Jack, and you guys come meet us. I'll catch up to the girls, and then you meet us there. Do you understand me?"

"Yes, but if I don't get going I'm going to be too late, and I'd much rather it be Jack and I then just myself against that fucker. Now get going and don't make any noise you don't need to. If anything horrible happens he's going to want to come after me next."

Traci gave him one last kiss, turned and ran to the tree line, headed to try and catch up with the girls. Isaac looked around the forest floor, kicking at branches until he found one that was thick and not brittle but not so heavy he couldn't get a good baseball swing with it. He gripped it, testing it against a tree, and then ran across the field the best that he could. He watched as Jack was being pursued by the man, and then winced as he saw the stick which was almost as big as a log fly through the air. He got sick to his stomach as it struck his best friend in the world sending him to the ground.

Before the man could kick Jack a third time Isaac screamed, "Leave him alone you piece of shit."

The man, still looking at Jack and head bent down, put his foot back on the ground and then twisted his head as awkward as a human could so that he could see Isaac sprinting with the stick. Isaac still had plenty of ground to cover and the stranger bent down, gripped Jack by the hair and dead lifted him off of the ground. The man brought the machete back, and Isaac winced as he lunged it towards his friend, missing him and embedding it into the tree a foot above Jack's head.

Isaac's legs almost gave way at the visual in his head of the idea of the machete slicing into Jack's torso. The very thought made him lose some of his speed. He took a deep breath and picked up his pace again, but before he could make it the rest of the way the man pulled what looked like a bowie knife from the inside of his overalls and pinned Jack to the tree with a forearm under his chin. He stabbed him in the shoulder. Jack winced, screaming, unsure if he could endure any more pain, which was when the man brought out a second knife and stabbed him in his other shoulder. Jack's arms were now useless to him and Isaac knew that from here it was going to be him against the stranger.

Jack cried in pain as he hung there, the only thing keeping his legs from giving out were the blades that were pointing to the heavens and would cut him if he let his legs give out.

Isaac pleaded from across the field, "Let him go!"

The man gripped one of Jack's limp arms, holding it to his cheek in an oh my gesture, mocking Isaac. Clearly fear was the least of the sadistic intruder's worries. Isaac stopped for a moment, watching. He wasn't stupid and knew this man was dangerous, more so than anyone he'd ever encountered in his short life. He watched his friend's face begin to grow pale. The man was lifting his arms.

"I'm gonna kill you god damn it if you don't leave us alone!"

This seemed to get the man's attention, the man quit what he was doing. He let go of Jack's arm and looked directly at Isaac and waited for him to come at him. He shook his head no and motioned for the young man to come. Isaac sprinted, waiting until the very last minute to bring the stick down. Isaac had never seen a man this big move so fast. Isaac couldn't believe it was happening even though it was. He looked down and saw the man had a giant mitt of a hand wrapped around his wrist. He spun Isaac in a circle, and right before Isaac was ready to fall, the killer slammed him into an ancient oak tree.

Isaac grunted when he hit the tree, and he hit it hard. Not for the first time that day his world spun, and when he tried to get up he fell back to the ground. He could feel warm, fresh blood trickling down his face. He tried rising up off the ground, gripping the stranger's leg, looking up as he gripped Jack's hair. The stranger lifted Jack's head, stared directly in his eyes and dragged the machete across his neck slicing it clean and deep. Blood poured down Jack's front, wetting his shirt until it clung to his chest, which was barely rising.

Isaac, still barely hanging on, hammered on the man's leg.

"What the fuck is wrong with you?"

Isaac cringed, as he took a hand getting it soaking wet in the blood. The stranger ran a finger in a cross over his forehead and then put two more on his cheeks. Isaac tried to back away from the blood that was pattering on the ground. The man stood to the side, running the blade across Jack's neck even further and sending a spray of blood onto Isaac. He got up from the ground, slipping at first, and bear crawled away as best he could. The stranger saw this and ripped both knives from Jack's now limp body, and when both of them were out he lifted Jack above his head. The stranger hurled his still bleeding body into Isaac, hitting him full force in the back and sent him off balance and sprawling back to the ground.

Isaac rolled over on his back and tried to push himself up again. The man walked forward, almost looking like he was marching. He pulled one of the knives behind his shoulder and brought it back down with nothing but bad intentions. Isaac felt a sharp pain. When he tried to turn his head a knife blade was next to his cheek, and he felt new blood now making its way out of the side of his head. He screamed when he touched it. Pain exploded through the side of his skull. He felt his ear and could tell that it was now in two pieces and the knife had sliced it cleanly open.

When his hand came away bloodied he felt an entirely new pressure to get his ass up and moving. He got to his feet as the stranger started walking, still armed with the second knife. Isaac ran until he could feel his legs fully again and then pushed into a sprint. He took the most difficult path through the underbrush he could find. He knew that if he had to duck down to make it through the giant son of a bitch would have to practically army crawl. Isaac ran for what must have been ten minutes before sitting and trying to catch his breath. He felt like his chest was going to explode, and he could feel burning in his legs. He did a self-assessment realizing the ear wound was really the only problem he had to deal with and knew there wasn't a hell of a lot he could do about it. He ripped off a piece of his shirt making a makeshift bandage around his ear. It looked more like a bandana, but the last thing he wanted was for his earflap to catch on a branch and rip clean off of his head.

Isaac sat waiting and listening for a minute. He was staring at the branches praying to God the monster wasn't going to just somehow materialize and be running at him. He waited a few more minutes before he decided the man chose to go an entirely different direction. The only problem he'd had with this new thought was the three girls were going to be on their own. He thought about having to break the news to Katy and Jack's parents, whom he'd known since he was in diapers, and he could imagine what his mother's face was going to look like. After a little more thinking, he figured on the upside the only person who would have her heart broken if he was caught was Traci.

Chapter 18

Saturday

Brandi and Katy sprinted through the woods the best they could. Brandi had a firm grip on Katy's wrist because more than once she attempted to run back to Jack. His screams echoing through the trees were enough to break her heart. When they'd ran half the distance through the woods to what they believed was a safe stopping point they did. Katy sat on a downed tree with her face in her hands.

"I can't believe we fucking left him. Who fucking leaves someone when this kind of shit is happening? Do we have no souls?"

"Hey, your husband, as much as you hate it, was being a man. You can't be more chivalrous than throwing yourself under the bus if it means saving the one you love. If he makes it, you are going to owe him some serious fuck time. I mean-"

"Okay Brandi, it might be a good silent time. Can we just sit here for a second? I'm almost thirty and we've been together for a while so believe it or not, having my legs open isn't the biggest part of our relationship. We've been together forever, we've had to deal with the good and the bad, we've seen each other at our sickest, and had to deal with family loss. We have love and yes, even though my husband is still a complete horn-ball he actually still is capable of sitting on the couch with me without getting himself all worked up each and every time. You should try it some time. It's actually a pretty fucking rewarding life to live."

"Wow. Look you bitch, I was just trying to make you feel better."

"Well, you fucking nailed it didn't you? Why don't we try the silence thing and when this is all over we can all sit around and talk about that one time at band camp when the stranger came out of nowhere and killed your fuck buddy. You remember him, right? Yeah, and we can have a nice, very stiff drink."

"Whatever. If we live through this I'm moving. This is the most fucked thing that I have ever had to deal with. This state can lick my ass when this is over. I do not make nearly enough at my job to stay here. I think California is screaming my name out loud at this point."

"You realize statistically if you live through this that there's a pretty good chance you'll be able to go your entire life with good odds of never having another killer come after you? I mean how often do you hear about the victim getting away only for them to come back and kill you later?"

"I don't watch the news, okay."

"Shocker. You are something, you know it?"

Brandi started to retort but the sound of snapping branches caught their attention and was growing louder and closer. The two girls looked at each other. Brandi went to say something, but Katy stopped her, "Shut the fuck up!"

Katy looked around the forest floor, trying to find something she could use as a weapon.

"You're fucking crazy. You really want to try and fight that son of a bitch?" Brandi said.

Katy looked up when she'd found a sturdy thick branch. "No, I'm going to trip that big mother fucker and when he's down I'm going to put the tip of this branch through his neck. Then I'm going to leave him for dead and go back to my husband and we are going to walk to wherever that damn farmhouse is and beg them for a ride and to call the police. How does that sound to you?"

"Better than running only to have him catch up to us and chop our fucking heads off one at a time. But here, this stick's better, you'll be able to jab this right into his neck. I think."

"You hold on to it. Once he goes down you come up and stab the fucker with it."

"I don't know if I can do that, Katy."

"Really? He chopped your boy toy's head off and has terrorized us since, and you don't think that you can fight back? What the hell is wrong with you, suck it up!"

"Fine, you do your part, and I'll do mine."

The footsteps were getting closer and closer. The two women each hid behind a tree breathing heavy and trying unsuccessfully to keep their hands from shaking. Brandi mouthed, don't miss. Katy gave her a sarcastic thumbs up trying to calm herself. They did not have to wait long and when feet appeared, Katy slid the branch in-between them.

Chapter 19

Sunday

Hardin looked around the clearing trying to guess where best to go. It was almost impossible to tell where they should look. Bynum sat watching the seasoned detective.

"So are you going to track them, sir?"

Hardin looked back at him. "I'm a detective, rook, not a fucking Navajo. There's a reason why we get dogs to come out here." He looked for the men who were standing around in the field looking for any signs. "Hey, Johnson, did you find anyone with a set of dogs we could use?"

He nodded. "Yeah, it's going to be a few hours unfortunately, but there is a K-9 squad that is going to come this way and help us out. It's the best we could do."

Hardin threw up his hands and Lambert could see the frustration on his face. He wasn't sure if he was so hell bent on it because of the killer out there or because it was something personal. Lambert didn't like putting stress like this on people, because he knew nine out of ten times, especially when it came down to missing person cases, they were already doing everything that they could to try and help.

When Hardin came from Colorado with the highest recommendations he'd actually felt bad for the man when another killer arose. He told him he didn't have to take lead on the case if he didn't want to, and maybe he could just consult with the other detectives. Hardin told him his personal needs were second when it came to needing to try and save the lives of innocent people. The chief could tell the man truly had a knack for the job, and he hated the criminals with the same hate Lambert himself felt towards the enemy in Vietnam.

Lambert walked close to him as he walked around kicking in frustration at the long grass.

"You doing okay there, Hardin?"

Hardin, who was usually pretty well reserved, especially with superiors, said, "Fuck no I'm not okay. There could be people out there still alive and the best thing we have is a few hours to get a dog. That's fucking ridiculous. Don't they know how precious two hours is? Shit, I'd take a halfway intelligent hunting dog at this point if it meant getting a lead on something quicker."

"If this would have happened closer to home that probably would've been something I could have helped you out with. I don't know anyone in these parts, I honestly don't think me and the family have ever came out to this park before. Can't say that I have a lot of desire to ever come back here again after what we've seen today."

Lambert was barely being listened to. Hardin was peering around the wood's edge.

"Yeah, I can see how something like this-"

When he trailed off Lambert watched him and saw he'd stopped moving around the field glasses. "You find something?"

"I don't know for sure, but it looks like it'd be worth a look at. You want to head up there with me to have a look around?"

"With my bum knee, no way. Take one of the boys with you. They can still jump fences and chase people down and still get out of bed in the morning."

Hardin nodded. "Yeah, you know it isn't getting any easier as we get older. You got a preference on who I take with me?"

"No, but if you want to take the most seasoned with you take Nulty. If you want a runner grab Bynum, that little fucker works a ten-hour shift and he still goes to the gym. There's something wrong about that. When I used to get off work I didn't go to the gym, but then again no one went to the gym back then. We kept ourselves busy enough to keep from getting fat without it."

Hardin left the chief still reminiscing on the good ol' days and headed over to Bynum.

"Hey, rook, let's go. I might have seen something over there, and I don't want to wait for those dogs. There's no reason wasting time when we don't have it to waste."

He nodded unsurely and looked back at the Chief, who was paying no attention to him at all.

"Bynum, let's go, shake a leg. The chief was the one who already gave me permission to head out and take you with."

"Why, did he say you could take me?"

"Simple, I hate to run, and he said that you were a hell of a lot more physically fit than Nulty or DeBryan."

Bynum smiled at this, nodding and realizing being fatter would mean he could be walking lazily through the field looking for impossible to find clues. He would have the benefit of being surrounded totally by police and have someone watching his back. He didn't want to come off badly, so he just nodded his head uneasily and checked his gun was secure. Hardin pointed to Bynum's chest.

121

"You got your bullet right?" Bynum stared blankly, missing the Andy Griffith reference. "Never mind. You are probably too young to even know what the Griffith show is."

The two walked into the woods and it did not take long for them to smell the body. "What in the hell is that smell?" Bynum asked.

"If I had to guess I'd say that it is another victim."

Bynum pulled out his pistol. "Are you going to shoot the victim, rookie? Put that stupid thing away. If you need it I'll let you know."

They walked around a pile of brush and saw Jack's foot sticking out. His shirt had turned brown from the dried blood and his neck could not have been more mangled from the machete. They walked around looking at him and heard a crack in the distance.

"Okay, rookie, now you can pull your weapon."

"What about the victim?"

"You mean the dead body? He isn't going to go anywhere anytime soon. You know how long I've been working on this? If that sick fuck is still out here we aren't going to pussy foot around and lose him. Now get your ass moving, and let's go."

Bynum practically walked on Hardin's feet. "Grow some balls, boy. You go that way and I'll go this way. We don't want crossfire to be an issue. If you see him I want you to take him alive if you can. Unfortunately there are a lot of dead bodies I feel still need to be discovered. If we take him or her out then we will never be able to give their families any closure. I don't know about you but I'd hate to rob them of that."

Bynum nodded and started running lightly in his direction. He stopped every twenty to thirty feet listening for the sounds again. He wiped at his brow. The day was turning into a scorcher and the humidity did nothing to help. His shirt was sticking to his back and making him uncomfortable, not helping make it easy to concentrate on the task at hand.

Bynum slid his gun in its holster, then pulled out his dip can and, as quietly as he could, slapped his thumb on it, getting the amount ready to stick in, under his lip. When he did, he almost felt an immediate relief from the nicotine made its way through his blood stream. A crack came from behind him and he jumped, spinning around and trying to pull his gun. The man with the mask stared for only a moment before gripping his arm. Bynum opened his mouth to yell, but the man used his other hand to slam the blade into one of his lungs and then the other. Bynum quivered, letting go of the pistol and trying to keep his balance.

When he tried to yell again the man shook his head slowly no and placed a finger up to the officer's lips, then to his own, making it clear no was the answer when it came to screaming aloud. The man dipped a finger in Bynum's chest injury and made a smiley face on Bynum's cheeks. When Bynum was ready to pass out, the man slammed his head into a branch protruding from the tree sending it into his brain and leaving Bynum standing there suspended in air, dripping blood down his shirt and onto his legs.

*****

Lambert watched with the field glasses as the two men disappeared, not liking that they didn't have more available bodies for such a task. He hit his radio twenty minutes into it.

"Hardin, Bynum, I want you to check in. I don't like having everyone split up like this. It isn't smart work."

Just as he was about to start assembling men, Hardin answered. "Hey, Chief, there was a noise out here so we split up hoping to gain more ground and to see if we could catch up to it. We weren't sure what made it, but didn't want to take a chance on losing our opportunity if it was him."

"Yeah, I can appreciate that. You didn't find anything then; I assume?"

"We found a body. I didn't want a bunch of people rushing up here if that son of a bitch was standing near watching and scare him off. I fear that he's gone though."

"It was probably just a damn deer. Bynum, did you not hear me when I said to check back in, damn it?"

When no one came back over the radio Hardin said, "Let me circle back around, we've not been at this too long he can't be too-"

Lambert waited impatiently. "Hey, Hardin, I think you cut out there son. Were you saying that you were going to go and find him?"

Hardin spoke but there was nothing in his voice that spoke of compassion. He said it as if he was repeating it off of a card. "Sir, I need you to get two gurneys out here to get people out of here on."

"What do you mean two....oh my god, don't tell me that you found Traci out there? Don't you tell me that, damn it!"

"No, no that isn't it, it's....it is Bynum. I don't know what the fuck happened, but the son of a bitch must be out

124

here. He killed him. The son of a bitch killed him, god damn it. If I'd have gone this way, and had him go the other, I would have finally been able to catch up to him. Fuck!"

"He got Bynum? Son of a bitch, he's just a kid. Fire off a couple shots. I want him to make sure we aren't dicking around out here. I'll have the men out here follow you and catch up. I don't want anyone else alone the rest of the day out here. You hang tight, and don't do anything stupid. I'm not going to lose any more men today. I mean that, god damn it!"

Hardin walked towards the edge of the woods to wait for the rest of the men, keeping a pistol by his side. He hit his radio. "I can't waste an opportunity like this. There looks to be a house in the distance; there is a smoke trail coming from it at the least. You guys meet me there. I'm going in to see what is going on. I won't do anything stupid, I promise."

Lambert came back on his radio, "Hey, it isn't your fault, you remember that. I'm sorry that I sent you in without more backup. I don't know what I was thinking. There wasn't anything so important in the field going on that the rest of the men couldn't have split up and assisted you."

"We all make decisions, sir, and it is something that we have got to live with, we just don't have to like it every time we make a decision we aren't in love with afterwards. I'll tell his parents if you want? I don't think you are going to find her, the killer usually doesn't hang around the kill scene. Once they move on they are usually gone."

"Do you think that he might be changing his kill pattern?"

"I sure as hell hope not, Chief. Before you get to

Bynum you are going to see another man. He looks like he has multiple stab wounds and a laceration across his neck. It is a pretty deep cut and there isn't a lot left of his neck to keep his head and body attached."

"You look at the house, and that is it. You don't do anything else, you understand me, Hardin?"

"Unless I see them walking around, then I'm not going to go anywhere, I promise."

"Like I said, we aren't going to lose anyone else today. You sit on that house, and stay there!"

"Yes, sir, Chief, will do. I had my wife probably tell me the same thing that yours told you before you left."

"What, that you are a pain in the ass?"

"Yeah, you know it was something like that, sir."

Chapter 20

Saturday

Traci flew forward, screaming as she hit the ground, and slid painfully through a thorn bush, twigs, and rocks. Brandi was trying to bring the stick down; she had her eyes shut, and Katy jumped across the battered Traci and tackled her around her stomach. Brandi hit hard, letting out a good deal of air.

"What the fuck is wrong with you, Katy?"

"Well, if you would have been paying attention you would have seen you probably didn't want to kill the person beneath you."

Brandi moved to the side so that she could see and took in Traci trying to get up from the ground, failing at first and falling back to the ground. Katy moved over and helped her up, slowly. Traci winced as she extended her arms. There was a bloody leaf angel beneath her. Her short shirt and tank top did little to protect her as she slid.

"Fuck me, I'm so sorry. Are you okay, Traci?"

Traci was still in shock. "I didn't think that I had any chance of catching up to you two. Isaac stayed behind-"

"What, why, what was he thinking?" Brandi asked.

"He was thinking that his best friend was about to be murdered right in front of him, and the idea of it was more than he obviously could handle."

Katy stared at Brandi coldly. "Hmm, sounds like I'm not the only one that was trying to use morals. I knew that I should have stayed with him but someone bitch slapped me and then pulled me into the woods leaving my husband behind."

Traci tried lifting her legs and rotated her arms to see what range of motion she had in them. She couldn't have been more pleased with the results but wasn't ignorant and knew sitting there complaining about things that couldn't be changed would do no one, including herself, any good. Traci looked at the two of them.

"Get me a stick, too. I am done being a victim. If that son of a bitch comes after me again I'm going to stab him through that stupid fucking mask of his and call the cops long after he's dead."

"Wow, this isn't how you act at the office, Traci."

"Really, Brandi? I also don't have a psychotic piece of shit running crazy in the office trying to kill me. Because I'd fucking kill them, too."

Brandi held out a stick for her, and the three of them headed to the wood's edge, peering out to see if there was anyone or anything they needed to be wary of or about.

"So once we call the cops did you want to go back and try and find Isaac?" Katy asked.

"If they have a gun or something we can borrow, or maybe knives, I don't know. There's a good chance that sick fuck could probably take all three of us out, but it is my man and I love him. Christ, I just got engaged today, and I have to worry about losing him already. Do you know how much bullshit that is?"

"Well, in a year when we are all somewhere tropical celebrating the wedding of you two we will be feeling extra thankful for the love that we all have for each other."

"You guys think that we could maybe talk about this later and get a move on? If things are so important sitting here and talking about it isn't doing anyone any good at all," Brandi said.

"She's right," Katy said. "There's about a million nicer ways she could have said it, but what are you going to do with some people's kids?"

Brandi went to say something, but the two of them walked ahead, leaving her standing by herself open mouthed. She ran to catch up to them, not wanting for one second to be by herself in the woods filled with killers. The girls walked to the edge of the timber looking around, waiting, and deemed it looked safe to go and venture out. They walked out onto the gravel driveway that covered most of the property along the edge of the barn. Katy was in the lead when she walked to the edge of barn. She looked both ways quickly to make sure the monster wasn't lurking around the corner. A scream tried to pour from her but Traci was there instantly, pulling her backwards and hushing her as she covered her mouth. She let go and said, "What.....what is it?"

Katy turned Traci around to face her, face void of all color. "It's a man. He's dead. That son of a bitch must have come here first. He doesn't look all that fresh either."

Traci peered around the corner, wishing she hadn't; the visual she received wasn't anything she needed to have in her memory bank.

"Could this day get any weirder?" Katy said.

The three of them avoided Steven and made their way across to the house. When they made it there they listened, hearing a screaming whistling sound coming from inside.

"Who the fuck makes tea when a dead man is

hanging outside?" Brandi asked.

"Maybe someone who was expecting a normal day yesterday or the day before? Maybe the killer put it on there before he left because he's all kinds of effed up." Traci said.

Katy gripped the handle of the door, checking the lock. When it opened, she pushed the old wood door open slowly, seeing the horror show before her. They looked down at the antique wood floor with the long blood trail leading outside and one heading up the stairs. They made their way in slowly and cautiously. Brandi opened her mouth to say something, and Katy shook her head no holding a finger up to her mouth. They walked the first floor of the house, checking doors. The home had no basement, and they were thankful as hell for that. When they made it to the kitchen, they removed the teapot and looked around; the new silence was almost deafening.

"Okay, so where's the fucking phone?" Katy asked.

Brandi pointed, almost laughing, at the wall-mounted line. "Oh my god, they have a home phone. Who even has a home phone?"

Traci walked to it quickly, avoiding the blood marks everywhere on the floor. "Really, you are making fun of the one thing besides a gun that could potentially save our lives?" She picked the receiver up off of the wall and listened for the dial tone. "It's dead, damn it. Let's check the rest of the house. Maybe there's something else up there that we can use. Maybe we can find a cell phone up there."

"Yeah, that or we are going to find another dead body. This place just screams that good things happened here," Brandi said.

"Well, maybe we'll find some car keys and we can just drive on out of here. I know it wouldn't break my heart if we put some distance between us and this place. Maybe we could find the boys on the way out. Wouldn't that be amazing? Let the cops send like a thousand guys here and find that son of a bitch and kill him," Katy said.

The three of them started to head towards the receiver when a lamp fell in the living room, followed by feet running wildly across the floor toward them. The three of them screamed as they sprinted up the stairs. Traci pushed them as fast as she could until she looked down and saw a black cat sprinting through their legs and to the safety of a room upstairs. They stopped, taking their time to laugh about it for a second.

"Anyone else feel totally fucking paranoid? Katy asked.

"Affirmative on that," Brandi said, still trying to catch her breath.

They made their way up the rest of the long staircase, looked around, and saw a row of doors, and a trail of blood leading to one they decided should be the last to be checked until they heard the cat hissing, sending shivers down their spines into their toes. They walked to the edge of the doorway and stopped short.

"Do you think that is the lady that owns this place?" Brandi asked.

"I sure as hell hope so," Traci replied.

"What do you mean by that?" Katy asked.

"Because if this isn't her house then there is a really strong chance that we stumbled on to his home, and I don't want to think about this being his place where he brings people to kill and torture. He must have killed her and left her like that."

Brandi went to say something, and Christy brought her head up trying to blink enough until she could see and scared the hell out of the girls. Christy looked like she was using every ounce of strength she had to hold her head steady. The amount of blood coming from the side of her head was not the worst thing about looking at her. They could tell that the woman had been tortured. She wasn't sitting up in the chair; she had been tied in a sitting position and each of her hands and feet had a single nail ran through them holding her to the chair and her feet flat to the floor. Small pools of dried blood had crusted.

"Oh my god. We need to help her. Are you okay? We are going to help you, I swear," Katy said.

When the woman went to talk they noticed she wasn't being shy. She had her lips sewn shut with heavy thread. They went to touch it, and she screamed. Katy looked throughout the room, saw the mannequin body in the corner with a half-finished dress on it and found a pair of scissors.

"I'm going to cut that string, is that okay?"

The woman started to cry, barely able to keep herself calm. Traci ran a hand down her face.

"It's okay, we're here now. We are going to take care of you, I swear. I need you to try and stay calm. I don't want to cut you. Can you sit still, please?"

When they realized she wasn't able to control herself Brandi and Traci did their best to hold her head steady; her wild eyes looked like she was about ready to pop the blood vessels in them. Katy did her best to cut through the string, getting as many as she could. She winced as drips of blood began to pour out from the woman's mouth. She could see the woman's gums; at first Katy thought she probably wore dentures. When she was done and the woman could open her mouth all the way, she saw he had pulled the teeth from her mouth. When Traci saw this she thought of the man they found.

"Is that your husband outside by the barn?" Traci asked.

Christy, who they were pretty sure was in some sort of shock, looked back between the three of them. The tears that had begun were now accompanied by snot and blood from her teeth.

"Jesus, would you please say something, lady? You are totally freaking me out," Brandi said.

Christy, who made little sense with a severed tongue, mumbled, "He's behind you."

Chapter 21

Saturday; Ten minutes before the girls found Christy

Isaac ran as hard as he could. Each time he pumped his arm the pain that ripped through his shoulder wound was excruciating. He knew no one was going to save him, and if he wanted to live he needed to move. He ran until he had to stop and puke. He leaned against a tree, holding on for balance and losing the drinks and small amount of food he had earlier. What had been only a few hours, now felt like it had been years.

He wiped his mouth with his free arm, when he tried to come up he fell to the ground. Extreme pain burned through his wrist. He pushed up with his left hand, not daring to put any pressure on his right. When Isaac looked up he saw his right hand in the hand of the stranger. He wasn't able to believe what was happening at the moment. He screamed and looked at his wrist. When he did he saw, yes, the hand was his, and it was no longer attached.

He tried to push himself up and fell back to the ground. The blood that was pouring from his wrist was sending him into a state of dizziness and feeling faint. He looked behind him and saw the stranger standing there drawing swirls down the blade with his blood. The son of a bitch was toying with him. Isaac pushed up to his rear and scooted backwards, ripping the belt from his side. He wrapped it around his wrist, tightening it until there was no give left, and put it through the loop to tie it off. He wasn't a doctor, but wasn't stupid and knew if he did not stop the bleeding that he wasn't going to be conscious in a few minutes.

The man waited patiently, playing with the blade, almost mocking him, and in no hurry. Isaac said, "You enjoy this shit don't you, mother fucker?"

The man nodded, giving a thumbs up enthusiastically.

"You know one day you aren't going to be so damn smart or so damn lucky, and you are going to have to deal with the repercussions of your choices. I pray for that lucky fucker's sake that they shoot first and ask questions second. I'm pretty sure that you have a one on one date with the devil in your very near future. What you don't know how to talk?"

The man bent down, getting very close to Isaac. He pulled up the mask and said, "I don't usually have anyone want to talk to me."

Isaac just stared at the man. "You.....you look normal. You don't look like-"

"Like a killer? I assure you I am." At that he pulled the mask back down, reaching forward and sliding the blade in through Isaac's stomach until it came out the other side.

Isaac tried to speak but couldn't. He fell to the ground, looking up at the clearing in the trees, watching as the clouds rolled past him, moving slowly on what he thought, ironically, would have been a beautiful day with friends and his love if this psycho hadn't ruined their day.

The stranger knelt down next to Isaac, patting his face. He leaned back, reached behind and grabbed Isaac's hand sliding it inside of his overalls. As Isaac slipped into darkness he watched as the stranger started to walk toward the farmhouse. In the upper window he could see the girls. Or thought he could see them.

Chapter 22

Sunday

The police made their way through the forest and very quickly found Jack still on the ground.

"Chief Lambert, you want us to get photos of this?"

"No son, we don't have time to waste here. We need to go and see if we can find this bastard before he tries to take anyone else out in our group."

"You aren't worried about the scene, sir?"

"If I did would I have told you otherwise?"

The man wasn't new himself and he was smart enough to just stay quiet and nod. He thought about it. "Ain't easy is it, sir? We've lost men before. We'll do our best to catch this son of a bitch, you make the call and we'll do the footwork. We aren't quitters here, sir."

Lambert gave him a thumbs up, looking around. "We fan out, if anyone, and I mean anyone, sees anything, you call it in. I don't care if you aren't sure if it's a killer or a rabbit. If you see something you report back. You don't try to subdue him. Are there any questions?"

One man, an obvious rookie to the department, raised a hand laughing. "Chief, we got Glocks for god sakes. This guy seems to be a pretty big fan of the knives. I think we can take him."

Lambert walked in a beeline straight for the man much faster than anyone had seen someone his age move in a while. The man tried to back up step, but it was too late and Lambert had him by the front of his shirt, lifting him by his Kevlar vest and tossing him a few feet backwards. The man tried to get up from the ground, and

Lambert punched him in the face twice, spilling blood from his lip and his nose. Lambert screamed, "That was two seconds you little fuck-wad. How's that gun doing? Still in place by your side, right? Let me repeat myself. Anyone at all sees him or her, whatever this freak is, you fucking call it in."

The rookie, not knowing to just leave well enough alone, said, "I'm gonna report this to my union rep. You can't do this shit."

"You go ahead and do that, son, and you tell Jeff that Chief Lambert said hi. If he looks at you funny just say Nick and the kids say hi. You got any other grievances you want to put out, or are you going to move on and help to catch this serial killer?"

The man went to speak and one of his superiors placed a firm grip on his shoulder, squeezing until whatever the man wanted to say had passed. The rookie nodded and they fanned out, pistols drawn. They took their time walking slowly, trying to be as quiet as possible. The branches painting the forest floor didn't make anything easy though. Lambert said, "Nulty, DeBryan, you get out there and see if you can catch up to Hardin. There's nothing smart about anyone running off on their own today. I got a feeling that he is feeling more than a bit guilty about Bynum, which I can't say I blame him."

DeBryan and Nulty nodded, they'd worked together for a decade plus and weren't new to this.

"We'll radio once we find him, Chief. I am pretty sure he can handle himself," Nulty said.

"Just because he's big doesn't mean that sneaky fuck can't come up on him. Look at Bynum over there on the tree if you have any questions, I'm sure he's in better shape than all of us."

DeBryan patted his midsection. "Well, if he gets me it's gonna be on the ground, he ain't lifting this man muscle up."

Nulty pulled him to get walking. "Yeah, your man muscle is from the unrelenting workout of twelve ounce curls. You could get a gold in the Olympics if it was a sport."

"Please, I'm already a professional in most bartender's eyes."

Lambert watched as his men disappeared into the woods. He walked the line, pointing people in the directions to go.

"We need to move on this, gentlemen. We've never had a chance to be in the same area as him. We only get day old kills and a nervous nine one one call."

The men all nodded and Lambert went with the last group of men fanning out over a hundred yards. He thought of his granddaughter Lisa and smiled, then he thought about his piece of pie and was sure the little shit had instantly seen a piece missing when she had invaded Tricia's kitchen looking for a snack of some sort.

Lambert hit his radio. "Hey, boys how you doing on the west end?"

Nulty came back over. "There's trees, sir. Lots of trees. We haven't seen anything yet. Don't worry, we'll report back if we see something though, I can assure you."

A branch snapped in the distance. "Sir we might have something. I'll stay live though. We need to get across this stream and see what it was." Nulty said.

"How far have you gone?"

"Sir, we've already made it at least a half mile. We take this serious. He got one of our own, sir," DeBryan said.

"You just make sure that you do."

DeBryan went to say something into his mic and it only came back as a choking sound. Lambert asked, "What was that son....son?"

Nulty turned around to look at DeBryan and felt his stomach turn ten different ways. DeBryan was standing, but it was only because of the giant standing behind him holding him up. His machete was dripping with fresh blood, and DeBryan's under belly had been cut from the left of his waist all the way across his belt line and to the back. Nulty whispered, "Oh my god!"

"What, what is it Nulty?"

"Him, sir. He's standing in front of me."

"Then shoot that son of a bitch. Shoot him right goddamn now!"

"I can't, sir. He's holding up DeBryan, and we are going to need a medic on scene now. He cut him across his beltline. I think that he can pull through though. I don't have a shot though, sir. He's using DeBryan as a shield."

"Then fucking move until you do have a shot. Damn it Nulty, we aren't going to fucking ruin this opportunity. You make something happen. You didn't see where he came from?"

"Sir, I don't think at this point and time it really makes a lot of difference does it?"

"No, I assume not," Lambert said, slowly thinking about how he could get to his men. He flicked his radio to medical on nine and reported to send two ambulances and a coroner's out to the scene to pick up the victims.

Nulty started to slowly circle, but the man kept DeBryan in front of him, stepping into a small circle. Nulty ignored the fact he was in one foot of water. Nulty had no clue about the man other than killing was his thing.

"Hey, it isn't too late. You can let him down and go in peacefully, and we can all live through the day. Why don't you put him down and come in? You don't want to kill anyone else do you?"

The man stopped walking and held DeBryan to the side for only a moment, nodding his head yes, he most definitely wanted to continue killing and that he was not done by far yet. DeBryan, who was just barely conscious from the blood pouring down the front of his pants, yelled.

"Would you fucking kill him already? Please shoot this son of a bitch and do it now, damn it!"

Nulty whispered as if only the two of them could hear it, "There isn't a shot, Mark, trust me I want to shoot him."

The man held up a finger waving it in a shame on you gesture. The stranger made the machete disappear behind his back and brought his hand back and ripped up the remaining skin that was keeping DeBryan's organs on the inside where god intended them to be. Nulty saw this and screamed, "No!"

He had a front row seat to his own snuff film. DeBryan's stomach emptied onto the ground in front of him. His intestines and stomach landed on the ground. His stomach, which had been quite full, now looked depleted of everything. The stomach fell to the ground puncturing on a stick and sending a rancid smell into the air, making

DeBryan and Nulty both begin to gag uncontrollably. The killer lifted a much lighter DeBryan and ran him into Nulty, who forgot he was in water that only got deeper as he tried to get a shot. DeBryan's weight was enough to knock him off of his feet. Nulty disappeared for a moment under the water. He opened his eyes and all he could see was DeBryan sitting on top of him, dead and growing cold with the water from the steady stream.

Nulty pushed him aside and came up for breath with his pistol still in his hand. He shot out of the water sucking in sweet air, which instantly burned his lungs. He looked where he thought the man would be and saw nothing but guts and blood on the ground. He turned his head to sit up fully and saw the man standing in front of him. He brought up his pistol to aim, wanting to at least get off a Hail Mary shot, but the man brought the machete down once cutting his hand off. Nulty screamed in agony he'd never before felt, and watched as his hand, still clenching the gun, floated down the stream.

Nulty's clenched his teeth saying, "Just fucking do it you piece of shit. Come on you coward."

The man knelt down, pushing Nulty down into the water. He held him there just below the brim of the water. Nulty became hard to see the further he put him in. Nulty's blood covered the stranger as he struck him with the stump of his wrist and the one still attached. Nulty's air supply did not last long before it started to slowly be released and then completely. The stranger stayed hunched over him until there was no life left within his body, stroking the hair from Nulty's face so he could see his dead eyes staring back at him. He let go of the officer's shirt and let him float away into the nothing.

****

Ten minutes later

Hardin sat on the edge of the woods watching the house. He hit his radio and said, "Sir, he just went into the house. I'm moving in, if you aren't close."

"We are trying to find DeBryan and Nulty. I think he might have gotten them."

"Send who you can, I don't trust this son of a bitch for a minute. If this is his house or someone else's, he's still got other exits to leave from. I'm not going to give him that chance. I can't lose him, Chief, not after all this. We can't go through everything just to end up losing him. I'm going in."

Lambert went to say something else, but Hardin hit his radio off button not wanting the chatter to come through. Lambert cursed as they were running through the woods in a mob of officers looking for the man. They stopped abruptly when Nulty floated past him. Lambert leaped into the water, stopping his officer's body and jumped when his hand floated past. He knelt in the water, not caring about getting wet. He hung his head as he pulled Nulty from the water and to the edge. He noticed the man had sliced two upward cuts on his cheeks giving him the forever impression he was smiling even into the afterlife.

Lambert pulled Nulty's body up to the side of the bank and said, "We get this fucker. We don't separate again for anything. We need to find this house, and we need to do it now. Hardin just went in cowboy with no backup and he needs someone to watch his six."

Chapter 23

Saturday

The three girls turned simultaneously around to see the uninvited stranger standing behind them. He took a step into the room, slamming the door shut hard enough that it shook the room. The three of them jumped.

Katy said, "That's it, we didn't get these sticks in the woods to sit here and wait for him to come after us!"

Brandi was frozen in place. "You better suck it up, Brandi, because he's going to fucking kill you if you don't." Traci told her.

Traci turned to the killer. "Why, don't you get out of here? We are going to call the cops, my fiancé is going to get here soon and he's going to whoop your ass."

Katy jumped in. "Yeah, my husband Jack is going to come for you, and then you better hope that they are merciful, you son of a bitch!"

The stranger pulled Isaac's hand out from his pocket and waved it back and forth saying hello. He tossed it at the feet of Traci, letting her see the class ring that was blood soaked and at the same time undeniable that it was Isaac's. Tears started running. "Oh my god....I....I think I'm going to be sick. Yeah, I'm going to puke. Did you kill him? Did you?"

The man held his fingers together an inch apart.

"What do you mean a little, you sadistic son of a bitch?"

The man looked at his index and thumb and slowly started to separate them apart until he held his hands a foot apart. Traci's shoulders started to slump.

"What about the other man? Did you kill him?" Katy asked, scared to get the answer.

The man slid a finger across his neck. The woman did the opposite of what he had expected to happen. Katy gripped her stick and sprinted towards him. Katy thought she had it figured out, but the man brought his machete out, and slammed the side of the blade to her head, knocking her off her feet and into the wall. Brandi stood there in shock, and Traci sprinted for the man holding the stick like a spear. The stranger gripped it, bringing her in towards him. He clutched her shirt, spun her around, and sent her out of the second story window. Traci screamed as she went backwards headfirst and disappeared from view. Traci landed on the awning under the window, leaving a bloody stain. The momentum sent her across the awning where she landed on the ground, breaking open the cuts that had clotted.

The stranger looked out the window and saw her on the ground still moving. Katy and Brandi ran at him trying to knock him out the window. The man brought back an elbow into Brandi's abdomen and when she hunched over, and grabbed her abs, the stranger pulled her head up and punched her in the face, sending her into the opposite wall. Katy tried to stab the giant in the chest with her stick but the stranger was too quick and snatched her wrist, dead lifted her, and carried her over to the window and threw her out of it. The stranger made sure this one had no awning and watched as she plummeted to the ground kicking and screaming. When she hit, it was hard and knocked her out. Her leg bent so far to the side he was sure it was broken.

A whimpering sound came from Christy and Brandi. When he looked at Christy he tilted his head to the side, seeing the piece of yarn on the floor dried and bloody. He shook his head no while pointing at it, and Christy tried to speak. "It wasn't my fault, I didn't ask them to cut it."

The man went to sit on Christy's lap when Brandi pleaded, "Please, please just leave."

The stranger bent down putting a finger to her mouth to shush her. She looked up shaking her head uncontrollably. When she tried to move his finger from her mouth the man brought the machete down as hard as he could. Her pleading stopped and Christy shrunk in her seat. The only chance she could see to be saved was now gone. The woman before her had the machete buried in her skull and protruding out of the back of her spine. The man glanced at Christy looking around the room. He put a hand on Brandi's shoulder, sliding the knife back out. Its crimson red color sparkled in the sunlight fighting to make its way past the curtains. She mumbled the best she could, "Please, leave me alone. Please."

He rubbed her head as he walked past to her bench of crafting and embroidery items. The stranger picked more of the yarn and brought it back. She was shaking and the tears would not stop falling. He rethreaded the needle then began to sew, taking it in and out again.

She tried to scream, but he had such a grip on her chin it made it almost impossible for her to do anything but utter sounds which made no sense. The stranger chose to make sure each hole he used to close her mouth again was new. Blood trickled from the new wounds, running over the scabs and down the stranger's fingertips.

The killer held the blood in his hands looking at it, letting it run down his fingers and twisting them, letting it make its way all around his hand until it dripped to the floor. The stranger came out of his fixation knowing he had his machete sitting on his lap Christy did her absolute best to lean in and try to stab herself with the blade. The stranger gripped her hair by the back of her neck, pulled her backwards and shaking his head no. He pulled her in giving her a hug and rubbing her back. The stranger checked that her hands were still secured by the nails, as well as her feet, and took the blood from her lips to draw a smiley face on both cheeks. He walked out slowly, waving goodbye as he walked out and closed and locked the door.

*****

Traci rolled to the side doing what she could to not pass out, including slapping herself across the cheek hard and fast. She had adrenaline and was confident she wouldn't live if she didn't get some more flowing into her bloodstream. She heard crying close by and pushed up, crawling at first until she saw Katy on the ground not moving. She got to her feet and trying to run but her ankle stopped that. She hobbled to her best friend's side. Shaking her gently.

"Katy...Katy it's me, are you okay? Do you think you can make it?" Traci asked shaking her gently.

"He'll just catch up again. Every time he does he causes pain. I'm surprised that we are alive at this point. I think I hurt my leg when I hit the ground. It isn't moving, I don't know if I can run on it."

Traci looked around. "There's a truck over there. We can take the truck; you just need to get over there. You can do it. I can help you. Let's go."

Traci took a grip on Katy's arm, helping to lift her to her feet and wrapping an arm around her shoulder to make sure that she wouldn't fall back down. Katy was right, Traci quickly realized, when she looked down and saw the amount of weight she was able to put on her leg was a joke. They hurried the best they could to the old Ford pickup truck and Traci practically shoved her in on the bench seat.

"Katy, you need to start the truck. Let me get the hood down and we are out of here, okay!"

"That sounds fucking great, Traci, best thing you've ever said."

Traci disappeared, and Katy began turning the key. She tried to get it to start, but it was no good. Traci yelled, "Give it some gas. These are old and they aren't going to start so easy."

She did, so and the truck came to life, white smoke erupting out of the engine and from behind. The hood shut and when the smoke cleared the stranger was standing there holding Traci down with one arm, her head on the hood. Katy screamed, unsure what to do. She knew she could leave her friend and save herself, drive until she was somewhere safe. Traci fought to push up off the hood. The man lifted her up, brought her back down hard, and slammed her into the hood until the fight slipped from her.

Traci looked to her right as she was slipping from consciousness, and she thought she saw a ghost running the best it could across the driveway. Right before she blacked out she saw Isaac run with everything he had left and slam into the man, knocking him off balance. Isaac collapsed on top of him. The killer gripped his hands around Isaac's throat, stood up, and reach for Traci as she got up from the ground and walked the best that she could away from view around the barn.

The stranger stood with Isaac in one hand and opened the hood with his free one. He lifted the hood, reached in, and ripped the spark plug cables free, killing the truck. Katy dropped her head on the wheel, thinking she could not feel any more defeated. The man slammed the hood down once, twice, and then a third time. Isaac screamed, unsure what to do after the first, but by the third the sharp metal was cutting into his neck and by the final slam his neck had split open. The stranger opened it one last time, slammed the hood, and gripped Isaac's hair and ripped his head clean from his body, letting it fall to the ground. The man threw his head at the windshield, leaving a splatter.

Katy pushed the door open and tried to hobble away. The man threw Isaac's limp body to the ground and ran after her, catching her as she entered the barn. He lifted her up and slammed her into a load-supporting pole; a bolt punctured her back and came out the other side. She looked down, woozy and tired, ready to die, and watched the blood turn her already dirty shirt darker and darker red by the second.

"Would you just kill me? Please, just kill me. You have already taken everyone and everything from me that I care about."

The man patted her head, shaking his head no.

"What do you mean no, you fucking idiot? Just do it,

just do it!" She screamed.

He patted her face, turning around to check that they were still alone, then pulled a small knife. She shook her head from side to side, rethinking telling him that she didn't care about dying. He gripped her firmly on her chin, slid the knife up under her chin. He then took a piece of steel wire through her cheeks, tying it off to keep her mouth from opening.

Traci was hiding beneath a tractor that didn't work but made a great hiding place. She was frozen in fear with the perfect view of Isaac and his dead eyes staring back at her. She looked at the ring on her hand, shook her head and hit her fists in the dirt. She knew if they all died this son of a bitch would get away with it. She tried to think of a reason to go on and to fight; the only thing left she could think of was hate and her parents. The long running idea in her head that a parent should never have to bury their children ran through her head.

She looked around one last time before scooting out from under the heavy tractor. Traci got herself free of it and did her best to hobble away, but could hear the screaming taking place in the barn. She wasn't stupid; Traci knew that it was Katy, unless....and this second thought was a horrifying one. The question was, is this where he kept the rest of his victims he wanted to play with and torture over time. She slowed down even more her ankle was throbbing and looked around, knowing the son of a bitch seemed to materialize out of nowhere, and saw no one. She stuck her eye to a hollowed out knot in the wood barn, and saw her friend dangling a foot off the ground with a steady stream of blood running down her front and dripping off the back of her leg as well. Katy, even in her final moments, was clawing at the stranger with no power left in her weakened arms. The stranger did not seem to notice her at all as he worked methodically. She could see that he was shutting her mouth with wire.

Traci took a step back, trying to tell herself she did not have a chance to survive even if she could think of something. She knew each plan they had used had gone to shit almost instantly. She looked at the front entrance, seeing a ladder that went into the rafters. Traci thought if she could hide there until he left to look for her maybe, by some slim chance, she could sneak down and get Katy off of the beam.

Traci climbed up slowly, her injuries from the day had left her a bloody wreck. She tried to climb without feeling the pain and had to stop twice on the ladder to make sure the spins didn't send her off of the side of the ladder. She did not want to make her final effort of trying to save her best friend useless by breaking her neck after falling off the side of the ladder. When she made it finally to the top, she rested for a moment before starting across the floor.

When the killer finished, he stood back to look at his handiwork. He tilted his head to the left and then to the right, nodding to himself in approval. He brushed Katy's cheek and pushed the hair away from her face. She shuddered as he did it, on the brink of passing out. He looked at what was once a white tank top now a ruined bright red painted with pain and memories that would never go away. He saw a black drum of old oil and dipped two fingers and painted a smiley face onto her shirt. She couldn't help but be repulsed and shake when his fingers touched her skin. He stared at her intently, not breaking eye contact with her, holding her chin still so she was forced to stare at him. She tried to close her eyes, but he opened them himself. Their moment was ruined as dust began to fall from overhead, making her sneeze. The stranger looked up, watching as a new small bit of dust fell. He climbed onto one of the vehicles, which looked to have been parked and forgotten long ago. He waited beneath the dust. Traci moved, then stopped, then moved again. When she thought she was far enough in the barn, a hand punched through the rotted wood gripping her. She clawed at it wildly, screaming, thinking that yes, these were the final minutes of her life.

She tried to pull away but the hand lifted her up and down as the stranger's arm came further through the new hole, lifting her tiny frame and slamming her into the floor. He used his free hand to punch away at the rotted wood floor until he had a hole large enough to slide her through. Traci, just barely conscious, thought that the dark hole she was being pulled through would be her entrance into a hell that would never end. She screamed as she went through, and the killer let her fall freely onto the rusty truck hood. He knelt down next to her, hushing her as she lay there crying. When she started to kick and punch wildly, he treated her like a whining baby, pulling her onto his lap and rocking her back and forth. Traci spit in his face, and he shook his head. That was most definitely a no-no. He gripped her hair and slammed her head into the windshield, cracking it and splitting her forehead across her hairline, not stopping until she lay limp and bleeding on the hood.

Chapter 24

Sunday

Hardin hit his throat radio whispering, "Hey, Chief, I want everyone here, and I want them here now! He's going into the house. He is armed and dangerous. He looks like he has a machete, but from the size of the son of a bitch he looks like he has a damn butter knife in his hand. Tell you what, I'm heading in. You guys just head straight towards the noise of the gunfire and that'll be me taking this waste of existence out!"

Lambert started running with everything he could. He could remember seeing the slightest amount of smoke coming up in the distance.

"Everyone, you follow me. You see some big son of a bitch and you fire damn it, there are no questions. We are three men down and have already found two victims. This guy has obviously lost his shit. I'm not taking any other chances. All of you men are going to see your wives tonight!" Lambert yelled.

The men said nothing, they just followed Lambert as he led the way through the woods. He yelled, trying to keep control of his breath while not slowing down.

"Hardin….Hardin damn it, you wait. You hear a door open or shut in the back and you let me know. You wait outside of that house. That place probably has a million places to hide. Give us five minutes and we can be there. Just wait Hardin, I don't need to tell anyone else's wife that they aren't coming back home."

Hardin didn't answer. He was quiet for five minutes,

which seemed to be the longest five minutes of Lambert's life. He kept trying to run through the decisions he'd made that day and asking himself what he could have done better to have not had any losses. Much like when he'd enlisted for Vietnam with Chuck, neither of them wanted to die, and both knew there was a percentage that was far greater than they liked saying they wouldn't come back from war, but it didn't make it any easier when they did lose someone.

When Lambert had convinced himself the reason he wasn't reaching Hardin was because he'd been killed in the line of duty, he was already thinking of having to tell the detective's young wife what had happened. Hardin crackled over the radio. He sounded like he was out of breath.

"Chief, Chief, how close are you? He just took out a victim. This blood is still fresh I don't know where the fuck he-"

"Hardin. Hardin, what, what is it, do you have a visual on him?"

"Affirmative. He's downstairs. He just went out the back, and he has a girl in tow. He's going into the woods with her."

"You hold steady, son. We'll be there any minute. We can get him and her together."

"Shit, sir. He just started a dirt bike. Fuck me, he just rode off with the girl riding over the seat in front of him. She looked pretty fucking banged up. Goddamn it, this sick son of a bitch is always a step ahead of us. I don't know what to do."

"You wait, and you don't move, that is an official order, and there are twenty men to say they heard me tell you. Don't go anywhere, I mean anywhere at all. You aren't going to catch up to a damn motorcycle anyways. If this is his stomping ground he must have some sort of knowledge of the place. I can only imagine the booby traps that shit could have set up. I can see the house now, come on down if you are sure the victim is gone, and we will finish this correctly."

"Sounds good, Chief. I'm sorry that this happened today, it wasn't my intentions when I called for backup."

"Well, if you wouldn't have called for help there is a good chance that you already would have been done. You stay put, I can see the house now."

Hardin met them at the front door. Hardin opened the door that had blown shut and slowly holstered his pistol and walking out with both hands first yelling. "Don't shoot, don't shoot. It is Detective Matt Hardin. I repeat, do not shoot. They went out the back of the house. They are on some old dirt bike. I don't know if this is his house, or the woman who was upstairs. It's a pretty sick scene up there, sir. I think this might be his final breaking point. He's never taken this many so quickly before. If we lose him today he might go full auto and not stop until he is caught and that could be a fucking blood bath. I can't see him being worse, but I don't want to present the opportunity for him to be able to."

Lambert looked around, seeing rookies still with their pistols raised. "If you don't fucking drop that gun and let that man out I swear to god you'll regret ever becoming a police officer."

"Sir, I'm sorry, I just...."

"You just what? You just don't know how to follow

orders. Are you a fucking moron, son?"

"No sir, I-"

"You can't take orders or talk, good god we are fucked. You stay in front."

"Sir?"

"If you are in front you can't shoot anyone but the perp, damn it."

The rest of the men started to laugh at his comments. He snapped around. "I'm sorry gentlemen, what part of us wasting time or you guys hiring an absolute moron is remotely funny? Come to think of it, I'm starting to wonder about all of you men."

Lambert walked off without giving any orders or looking behind him to make sure that their guns had been holstered. He knew they would have been by now or this department really was useless. When he got up to Hardin, he patted him on the arm.

"You stay where I can see you from now on, you hear me kid?"

Hardin nodded, pulling out his pistol again and motioned. His radio beeped.

"What!" Hardin asked.

"Sir, it's Sergeant Adair. I have good news for you, sir."

"I doubt that with the way today is going. What is it? We are getting ready to go into the woods...again."

"The dogs just showed up that were requested, sir. The man in charge of them paid out a few favors and was able to get a flight in here. We can be there in five minutes by car.

"Do it, we will wait. Those dogs' noses will save us

any amount of time we would be willing to waste running through the woods trying to smell exhaust from a motorcycle."

"Yes sir, I'll radio one of the men to go get the address. We'll be in there in absolutely no time."

*****

As the men were beginning to grow impatient waiting for the police to come, a squad car came skidding into the gravel driveway and slid to a stop. The trainer opened the door quickly, giving the dogs a command that only he and the dogs could hear. They started to circle around the chief. Lambert didn't need a bullhorn, or to cup his hands around his mouth; he could project his voice without any assistance.

"I know it's been a long and trying day, and we are all tired. This is the closest we have ever gotten to catching this son of a bitch. We are not going to come this far only to fail now. We are going to follow these dogs and catch the bastard. The girl is our first priority. We will bring her back out of these woods healthy as we find her and in one piece. She's my goddaughter, and I'm not about to lose her now. Is there anyone who doesn't understand any of this or has any questions?"

Not one man raised his hands, and someone handed the dog handler one of what they assumed to have been Traci's shirts. The dogs took one sniff of it and went to work. The chief watched expectantly, thinking they would have found the scent immediately but never having to work with dogs like this before didn't really know what to expect.

"Well, Hardin, what do you think, is she alive?"

"Honestly sir, he or she has changed something. She statistically has already survived longer than anyone else ever has. He might be evolving into something else. I'd hate to know what a serial killer ends up changing into. I think we both know that it isn't going to be a good thing. The only thing that ever ends their killing sprees is them being killed or caught. It's a psychological disease that they can't help, even medicated they still might be dangerous."

"I'm very sorry, but are you trying to say we should fucking feel sorry for them? You think that we should try and cure them somehow?"

"Yes sir….yes sir I am. And I got the cure right here." He held up his pistol. "And it is prescribed as 230 grains at .45 inches across as often as needed or until the magazine is empty."

The chief nodded at this. "Alrighty then, I guess the two of us have the same ideas. I'm not taking this bastard in though, I hope you thoroughly understand that. DeBryan, Nulty, Bynum. Christ he took half my damn staff in one day. My office is going to take years to try and recover from this."

"Unfortunately, Chief, it happens. We aren't trained to deal with people like this. I think that we should be thankful for at least one thing th-"

"What the hell do we have to be thankful for after losing three of my men? I'd love to know what those college brains of yours are thinking."

"Simply said, he uses a machete most of the time, or some sort of blade right?" The chief nodded and Hardin continued, "Imagine what this monster would do if he walked around with a M-16 or an Ar-15 or, god forbid, he figured out how to get any type of automatic weapon. He could go on a killing spree with no elegance to it at all. But he is picky, and he waits. He is smart."

"I don't know if smart is what I would call it, Hardin."

"The person has gone months on a spree and this is the first day anyone has actually seen the suspect."

"You seriously still think after all this there is still a chance in hell that it is a woman?"

"You can't rule things like that out."

"I don't know. I guess not, especially with all those freak cases that you know about. I'm glad we have you around to look at both angles on it."

"Chief, this isn't probably the best time to say this; if we get this guy today, I mean he lives or dies somehow, I'm done. My wife has been all over my ass lately about looking for something in the private sector and moving somewhere safe where the stress of the day doesn't follow me home like a shadow stalking my brain every night."

The chief thought about this and remembered waking up with nightmares for the first six months when he and Chuck had done their final tour in Vietnam. He could still imagine exactly what every single man looked, smelled, and sounded like in his company.

"Yeah, I can appreciate that Hardin. I just hope that between this guy and the one in Colorado you can un-see what you are being haunted by. I can't put up much of a fight, son. If I was you and so young, I'd probably take a different career. God knows the private jobs make more money anyways, and typically you don't have to be worried about everyone you go after trying to kill you."

"I don't know if it's too late or not sir, but I'm willing to try and keep my shit straight for a while not chasing after someone. It isn't easy on the brain having to deal with chasing someone for so long to finally catch them and feel a nothingness afterwards."

Lambert just nodded. He didn't think he was doing the man any good bringing up killings and visuals that would haunt him. Lambert could sense he wasn't the one who needed to be discussing this with him anyways, and there was a pretty good chance if this kid wanted to totally be fixed, he was going to have to talk to someone on a couch about things.

They walked for another mile, watching the two K-9s running back and forth sniffing, finding a trail, running for a bit, and then running back and forth again. Lambert walked up close to the man.

"Hey, my man saw them ride off on a dirt-bike. Shouldn't these dogs just be following a straight path?"

The man shrugged, using a clicker as he walked. "You want to let them know how to do their job?"

"Look, this is serious shit here. Every minute is-"

The two dogs started barking insanely and sprinted into the distance. The handler left him still finishing his sentence and sprinted after the dogs. He screamed commands in German only the dogs were able to understand and the dogs finally slowed down. He caught up to them, giving them both a treat and a back rub for doing a good job. The two dogs ignored the food. Their teeth were showing, and they were ready for blood.

The rest of the officers caught up within a minute, and Hardin walked as close as he dared. When he made it, he saw Traci and the suspect. Lambert showed up a few minutes later not able to do the run the younger officers could. He was panting and said, "Where....where is the motorcycle at?"

"Who gives a shit? There's the perp," Hardin whispered.

Lambert took off his cowboy hat, wiped at his brow, trying to think of something he could say to Traci to make her feel better and put her at some sort of ease. Of course there was nothing he could think of that made any sense at all.

"Traci, are you okay honey?"

Traci, who felt like she'd been in a daze, tried to shake her head free to where she could even speak. She nodded slowly, and then shook her head no.

"Get me out here, Uncle Nick. Get me out of here, please. I just want to go home. I just want to see mom and dad."

"Honey, where's Isaac?"

Hardin put a hand on his shoulder. "Sir, we need to deal with the bigger picture."

Lambert nodded, knowing the answers he was going to get would do nothing about getting this horrible standoff over. Lambert watched as the girl's legs quivered even resting on the ground. She had a shotgun taped to her neck by the barrel and the suspect had a shotgun in his hand duct taped as well. "What the fuck does that mask mean? Is that a dolls face?" Lambert whispered.

"I have no clue. It could be as random as him picking it up during Halloween last year when he began these murders. The cross though on it, looks like he added it.

Maybe he thinks that he is sending people to heaven? Maybe he is just a sick fuck. I'd probably think that answer number two is pretty god damn accurate."

"What do you want to do? That freak has his hand taped to that trigger, and if we take him out then what?" Lambert asked.

"Yeah, Traci's head disappears in an instant and becomes no more."

Hardin walked forward in front of the line of fire. "Look, you can still make it out of here. You don't have to die today. You let her go, and we can get you help, we can do something for you."

The masked one started to wave his arm, screaming towards them. "I don't know if he can talk?" Lambert said.

"I woke up like this with this taped to the back of my head. Get me out of here!"

She couldn't turn her head in any way to see who was behind her. "Do you know if the masked person is man or woman?" Lambert asked.

"Does it fucking matter? No, I don't know. It's the entire point of the mask! I'd guess a guy with how strong they are."

Lambert looked at the person behind and realized the jumpsuit could have been masking some serious muscles but had been expecting a much bigger person, but he'd also expect the person to half look like a monster as well. He wasn't stupid and knew there was a very good chance the killer could look like any of these officers. "I thought you said how big this son of a bitch was? Christ, he's smaller than you and I." He whispered to Hardin.

Hardin turned giving the chief an eye fucking the

163

chief wasn't used to getting. "Sir.....I'm quite confident that there are much more important things going on right now that has to deal with the life of your goddaughter. I'm sorry if in the stress of a moment I miscalculated the fucking suspect's size. I'm quite clear now I can hand point him out and give you a much more accurate description!"

"You give up now and I promise you that you live," Lambert said.

When Hardin stepped toward the masked suspect Traci said, "No, no you can't come closer. He'll shoot me!"

Traci moved forward just enough that the taped trigger pulled and a blast erupted across the forest. The men who had been surrounding them were instantly painted with skull, blood, brain matter, and pieces of her face. The men all fell back, momentarily picking pieces of her off of themselves. Lambert dropped to his knees, watching his goddaughter now headless fall to the ground, a bloody stump on top of her neck staring back at him.

"Nooooo, Traci! Oh my god, noooo. Shoot the son of a bitch. Shoot him right fucking now!"

The suspect held up his hand, now free, trying to tell them to stop but still unable to speak. They fired off thirty shots riddling the body with new holes and when they started to stumble to the side could see a metal cord. One that was attached to the tree and to the back of the killer. Lambert saw this first and yelled. It was as if he was back in Nam.

"There's a bomb, run for cover, do it now!"

The grenade blast was massive and he was sure there was more than one of them. The tree it had been tied to exploded, sending pieces of wood shrapnel in every direction. Lambert felt a burning sensation erupt through his thigh and screamed as he fell to the ground. Blood began to pour from his leg. He rolled to his side ripping out the tree fragment and stuffed it with a handkerchief that he always carried on him. He wanted to scream, but with the crying coming from around him and the visuals it was all he could do to not lose his mind.

He looked around seeing young men dressed in blood-covered clothes on the ground. Some was their own; much was from others. He crawled to the first man he could and began emergency triage, seeing what was wrong and then doing what he could to fix it or at the least put a temporary stop. The tree had been decimated and he was confident whatever was left of the killer would need to be put in a baggy. He looked back as he worked, seeing absolutely nothing left but the mask now burnt, bloodied, and torn that had been blown off in the force. Hardin was sitting next to a tree with his head in his knees. A slow trickle of blood came from his forehead.

"Hardin.....Hardin, Hardin, are you okay? Are you okay, son? Say something, damn it!"

Hardin looked up in a daze, unsure what to say. He shook his head yes, then no, then shrugged.

"This isn't how I wanted it to end. This isn't how I wanted things to happen. We were supposed to save her. We were supposed to bring her home, god damn it! It was a trap. The entire thing was a trap. He wanted to finish it this way and must have wanted it to be over but on his terms."

Lambert knew there wasn't anything he could do to make him feel better and because of that said nothing. He went around to the rest of the men, splitting the group basically in half with another man, the only other one that had been in the service and knew how to apply emergency medical care to this degree. Within twenty minutes they had everyone who was alive resting comfortably and waiting for the emergency techs to get back into the woods and see the bloody mess that was their job to deal with.

When the blast had gone off a local farmer heard it and came over on a four-wheeler instantly. Hardin and Lambert helped get the injured officers on the man's four-wheeler, and he chauffeured them out to the waiting ambulances. They were the last to make their way out, letting everyone else go first. When Lambert had gotten his leg stapled shut after the wound was cleaned out he ignored the urging of the emergency medical techs to come to the hospital. He hobbled away followed by Hardin who also was trying to convince him to go to the hospital.

"Sir, at least we got the son of a bitch. What else are we going to do? We aren't going to find anything else that we need to know today."

The chief ignored him and walked around the house. He went through the kitchen, seeing blood, then walked up the stairs following the bloodstains. He saw Brandi sitting in the back of the room in the corner, dead and crumpled. He saw yellow numbers everywhere for blood drips, and other identifying evidence. They found her purse in the flipped SUV and her ID was inside.

"So where the hell is the third woman? We are missing someone. This is Brandi, I find it hard to believe Jack Wallen's wife didn't accompany him on a holiday drive to a state park. Her car was parked out front at the apartment of Traci Pendergast's from what Chuck had told me. So where the fuck is she? The killer's gone, and there is no sign of her anywhere. There isn't anyone to ask."

Hardin stared at the scene, "I'll put it out that she is still missing but this forest expands forever. I know the dogs are still here. We can keep them running until their paws bleed if it means closure for her family."

Lambert opened his mouth to say something, and the horrible realization he still had to face Chuck and Rosa made him physically sick thinking about it.

"I know it's a bad scene, Chief. You really don't have to be here though. You can go to the hospital."

"I don't need a fucking hospital. I need a stiff drink and a fucking smoke."

He walked back downstairs and through the kitchen, seeing there was a pack on the counter and a zippo, and searched through the fridge until he found a bottle of vodka in the freezer.

Hardin found him lighting up and pouring a shot. "Sir, are you sure that you should be doing that?"

Lambert pulled a second cup, filling it with three fingers in each. He slid one to Hardin straight faced.

"Well, then I probably shouldn't drink alone. One drink isn't going to hurt a damn thing."

When Hardin didn't step further into the kitchen, Lambert clinked the second glass and slammed back one then the other. He put his head down on the counter, waiting for the burn of the alcohol to make its way through his body.

"Are you okay, Chief? You feel better now?"

Lambert pushed up off of the counter, spun around and threw the glass as hard as he could against the wall. It shattered, sending pieces everywhere.

"I need to go. I need to break the news to my best friend's family. Waiting isn't going to do anything to help and the last thing I want them to do is sit there thinking there is still a chance to have their daughter come back to them."

"Did you want me to go with you? I can help break the news?" Harding asked.

"No, you go home to your family and be thankful that you have got one. I'm sure after your wife hears about this bloodbath she'll be thankful for you to come home."

"You going to take care of the other officer's families as well, breaking the news?"

"Yeah, it's part of the job, son. It sure as hell isn't something I'm looking forward to. I'm going to see if I can get a ride back to the city."

"I'll give you a ride, come on. You don't need to drive after that anyways. I promise we don't have to talk. I won't try to make you feel better. I'm confident we aren't going to feel better for a long time to come."

They got a ride back to the park and Lambert and Hardin drove back in silence. By the time they made it back to the police station, Lambert was definitely ready for another drink. He patted Hardin on the shoulder, got out and said nothing as he walked to his truck.

He drove in silence to the Pendergast's home, running the conversation through his head for what seemed a million times over. When he pulled up to the front of their home, Chuck moved the curtain to see who was here from his recliner. He knew god damn well the news before his best friend ever made it to the door. He told Rosa to stay inside and went out to the front to meet Lambert.

Lambert was walking in a daze and Chuck's heart broke for him and for the news he knew was coming. Nick looked at his friend with tears in his eyes. His emotional limit had been reached and seeing Chuck's tired eyes had been his breaking point. He walked up and gave his friend a hug, a long one.

"It's okay Nick, I know you did everything you could. I know you did your best"

"Chuck, I don't know what to say, brother. We did everything we could. That son of a bitch was waiting for us. He took three of my men.....three of my good men out today. I just don't know what to say. We got him though, but unfortunately it was too little too late."

Chuck pointed down to Nick's pants. "Is that your blood, Nick?"

"The killer was rigged with bombs. After he shot Traci we unloaded on him. I'm sure it will come up as police brutality somehow by the fucking liberals if there would have been some way to account for how many shots he took. But I don't feel bad about it. Not for one goddamn moment. When he fell over a bomb that he had rigged to the tree detonated and I took a piece of wood in the leg. Three more men were killed from the blast. Pieces of the tree shot through their necks, ripping them in half and leaving them to bleed to death. There was nothing we could do to help them. "

"But you got the son of a bitch? He won't be able to hurt anyone else?"

"Yeah, when I say there isn't anything else left of him

I am not saying that subtly. That bomb fucking destroyed him completely. Traci's friend Katy is still missing. We have a APB out on her, but I'm pretty sure after everything that I've seen today that she's dead. God knows how, but dead is dead, and if she's gone the pain is over for her. Is there anything I can do for you, though?"

"No brother, you go home to Tricia. I'll let you know what details there are later and when the services will be. I appreciate you trying. It was all that you could do, and I know you did your best."

"It won't ever be enough. This is going to be waiting for me every night for as long as I can imagine."

Chuck went to go inside.

"What are you going to do now?" Lambert asked.

Chuck turned around, and he looked like he'd aged ten years in a matter of five minutes. Tears were starting to roll down his face.

"I'm going to go and break my wife's heart and tell her we won't ever see our baby again."

Nick nodded slowly, knowing there wasn't anything he could say to make anything better. Chuck tried to smile, but the face he made actually made Nick feel worse, which wasn't something he thought he could feel right now. As he walked slowly to his pickup both Rosa's and Chuck's screams and cries poured out from the house. The block was filled with the sounds of horror and sadness and grief all put together in one terrible orchestra of emotions.

Chapter 25

Tuesday

"Thank you for joining us today on this occasion. I know this is heartbreaking for many. No one wants to be thinking about how temporary our life is. I would be sad and I would feel sorrow if it was not for the fact that I know Traci Pendergrast is resting with the angels of heaven. She feels no pain and has no fear. She is smiling in the heavens, watching us from above. Please join hands as we send the final blessings to God above. Even though I walk through the valley of the shadow of death, I will fear no evil, for you are with me; your rod and your staff, they comfort me."

When the preacher finished his speech Chuck helped Rosa to her feet and walked her to the casket almost in a dazed state. Rosa knelt next to the coffin, giving it a kiss. They stood next to each other as workers slowly lowered it to its final resting place. Chuck and Rosa both dropped a white rose on top of it. Rosa's shoulders began to shake and Chuck did what he could to console her. He had been telling himself over and over again for the last few days it was not too late to grieve when this was done. He knew he needed to be a crutch for Rosa, but didn't know if his heart would be able to handle any more pain. He did not know if his mind could handle that.

When the funeral was over, those in attendance gave their condolences. They could tell just by looking at the couple that there was nothing they could possibly say to make them feel any better. Rosa had been sick of people telling them how Traci was in a better place, how she would feel no pain. She didn't even have the opportunity to see her baby whole before being laid to rest.

She had fought back and forth with Chuck and Nick to see her daughter. The two of them were adamant when they told her whatever way she could remember her daughter was better than trying to remember what was left of her now. The blast had been horrible and left nothing positive of her daughter to remember. In the end she decided the beautiful daughter she could remember was better than trying to add fuel to the guaranteed nightmares that would haunt her until the end of her days.

Lambert came across to shake Chuck's hand and when he came to Rosa gave her a hug and kiss. Tricia gave her a hug as well. She was an emotional wreck over what had happened, and it wasn't so much about the loss of Traci but the idea, that at any given moment she could lose one of her boys, or God forbid her grandchildren.

Later, when the people who only came for the service had gone, those left sat around reminiscing about Traci's life and all the good she had done. Rosa had got even worse when Traci's personal belongings had been returned to them and there was an engagement ring she never had the pleasure of sharing in the joyous news.

Nick came up to hand a beer to Chuck and patted him on the shoulder.

"Chuck, how are you doing, brother? You look like shit. Did you get any sleep the last few days?"

"Yeah, I sleep like a baby for about twenty minutes until the nightmares set in and then after that I wake up screaming in a cold sweat. I go out to the kitchen and get a glass of water. I'm old, so after that I go try and take a piss for another five minutes. Then I start the process over again."

"A simple no would have worked. I'm sorry man, I just want to say something. I just don't know what else-"

"Jesus Christ, Lambert, right now isn't the time to talk about this. Today isn't the time to talk about it. If you keep apologizing for this I'm gonna knock your ass out. I can't have this extra emotional stress right now, do you understand me?"

"You know that'd be assaulting an officer of the law, right?"

"Your wife would stick you on the couch for a month if you tried to put me in jail."

"One month, are you kidding me? I'd have to buy a damn air mattress. I'd never make my way back in after that. I just feel horrible."

"That just means that you have a soul, Lambert. Not that I ever questioned that before. Why don't we go into the garage, that's where I keep the good stuff. If I pulled out a bottle today Rosa would have my balls in a vice."

Nick followed him out to the garage, and Chuck took a bottle of Maker's Mark down, blowing the dust off of the bottle.

"I've been saving this. Originally it was for a special occasion, but I need something to dull the pain."

"You know a shrink would probably tell you that isn't healthy behavior, Chuck."

"Well, fucking lucky for me I'm not seeing one nor will I, damn it. I don't care what Rosa says. The bastard that killed her is dead, and that's all the closure I need. If I feel pain, it's because I loved her and that's what you are supposed to feel. I don't need a head shrink quack telling me I'll be better over time. The only thing that is going to make me feel any better is when I'm dead and I can reunite with her in heaven."

Lambert held up a glass and did the sign of the cross. He thought about the son of a bitch and couldn't get the mistakes out of his head, the tripwire attached, the explosion going off, the duct tape around them. It just didn't add up. Serial killers didn't tire of killing, that is how they became serial killers. Chuck was staring at his friend and after knowing him for more than forty years he knew he wouldn't let anything go. "Do you need some help clearing out their place?" Lambert asked.

"No. I already talked to their landlord, Peter. He said we could have as long as we needed. I asked for a week, and then we'll go in after that and clean it out. I can't imagine the two of them having too much shit to go through."

"Well, I think you might want to think about that. There might be a good chance they can collect more stuff than you can imagine."

"No, we will be okay. I'm going to donate all the furniture to the Goodwill; we have all we need and more now."

"There isn't any reason at all to give yourself more things to remember her by."

"I don't have any problems remembering her. This is one bad memory where I have a million good ones. It is just this one time, which is enough to haunt me for the rest of my life. Someone so beautiful, so wonderful, is going to leave me dreams that I cannot find a way to get rid of. I never thought that after Vietnam there would be a reason to have to deal with this again."

"I don't know, brother, but you let me know if you want any help. I know Tricia and I can take off any time we need to, to come and help."

"I appreciate that, Nick. I will take you up on that though more than likely. I'm no use when it comes to packing up kitchen shit. If I do it wrong, then I won't ever hear the end of it from Rosa. Because it's a crime to not properly wrap some dishes just so a dumbass minimum wage immigrant can go and throw half the shit and break it anyways."

Chapter 26

Two weeks after burial

Rosa had been collecting boxes for a week from the grocery store. Chuck went through his shop, grabbing a toolbox to take with them to disassemble bed frames and anything else they might want to take apart to make it easier to get things ready for when Goodwill showed up. Rosa came out to the shop.

"Chuck, are you ready to go? I don't think we can put this off any longer."

Chuck was moving a screwdriver back and forth in front of him at the workbench. He had the thousand yard stare she hadn't seen since he had come back from Vietnam when she was barely of drinking age. She remembered the night terrors, not being able to sleep, being tense and cranky.

"You know this doesn't have to be like when you came back, honey."

Chuck, who'd been snapping for a week, said, "I swear, woman if you bring up going to a fucking shrink-"

Rosa slammed the garage door and marched to her husband, and put her hands on his shoulders. He was still looking at the screwdriver. Rosa took it, put it in the toolbox, and closed it. She lifted his chin.

"You aren't going to go back down that road. You and your mind aren't old enough to come back from it. You need to let it out. You need to mourn, to cry, to let your heart break, honey."

"Has crying yourself to sleep made you feel any

176

better? Is your mourning process going easier because of it?"

"Yes. Do I still miss her each and every day? Of course I do, Chuck, but that pain hurts a little bit less. Not a lot, but a little, and moving forward is what we have to do. She wouldn't want you to be killing yourself every day over it. It isn't your fault. She was probably living the best day of her life from the size of that beautiful engagement ring."

Chuck closed the toolbox whispering, "She probably thought she had….that she had….had her entire life in front of her."

Chuck met his breaking point. Rosa pulled him in, letting his head rest on her chest, and brushed his hair as the tears began to fall down his face.

His shoulders shook and she whispered, "It's going to get better, baby. I swear it."

Chuck gripped her hard, crying so he could barely be understood. "It just hurts so much? She was so young, Rosa."

"I know she was. You are taking the first step in a long process. Come one, let's go over there and get the place cleaned up. It'll do us some good to do something besides sitting here and looking at each other. The landlord is only going to be patient for so long."

Chuck pulled a handkerchief from his pocket and wiped at his face and nose.

"That son of a bitch won't say anything as long as he keeps getting the checks. I already sent him an extra check for her rent to give us all the time that we needed. I wasn't sure if I'd be able to go in there or not. If you want to figure out their dishes and box those up, I'm going to go through all the paperwork and get their bills in order. I'm just going to pay for everything. I'm not sending all those bloodsuckers their death certificates. We pay it, we are done."

Rosa patted his back.

"You know they will write that stuff off if someone passes away, especially like this. There is usually a no questions asked policy. I read through the information we received at the funeral home on how to help deal with loss."

"Let me grab the truck keys, and we can get going. Do you have all the boxes you think we'll need?"

Rosa said, "We will probably need more, but that is just a matter of time. We can only fit so much in there before we need to take it all back downstairs."

"The Goodwill people will bring some, you just fill it up and they will take it. I doubt it will take that long to go through paperwork, then I'll start taking down the beds and lamps so it'll be easier for them to get it out the door. I just want everything taken care of and handled. The more things we put past them the easier I think things will be."

Rosa kissed his forehead. "Honey, are you telling me that, or are you telling yourself that?"

Chuck gave her a long hug. "Mostly myself. I think you are handling this the way people should. I'm handling it like-"

"There is no perfect way to handle these things, Chuck. You are an old stubborn marine. I wouldn't expect anything else from you."

They made their way into the apartment, already having a spare key. Rosa and Chuck made a few trips up and down to the truck getting all of the boxes she had been stashing over the last week. Chuck went to their file folders and tossed them on the coffee table, separating Isaac's from Traci's. He went through hers finding nothing but a few small bills from a few nothing companies she had credit cards for and then started looking through Isaac's finances. He was shaking his head trying to figure out how the boy made a living.

"Jesus Christ, I can't believe our daughter was going to marry someone who was this disorganized. It looks like he spent most of his money every month on that damn wedding ring."

"Well, him wanting to give our daughter the best isn't necessarily a bad thing is it, Chuck?"

"No, but being able to eat is more important than a ring."

"Not to a young woman who has been waiting for years to get an invitation to get married. She had subtly hinted more than once to me she was more than ready to settle down. She loved that boy, Chuck, more than she ever loved anyone else. She was the best thing that ever happened to that boy after he lost his own parents. I don't think he ever thought he would have someone love him again."

"Well, he lucked out getting our Traci. I'll stop talking bad about him. Sorry, honey. I ought to know better."

"You don't want bad karma, honey. If you need any help going through all that paperwork you let me know and I'll be happy to take a break. I think I'm going to have to call Tricia up after all, there's so many cups I think I could wrap them up for hours."

"Nick said she'd be happy to help. They are feeling as horrible as we are. Especially Nick."

"She told me he isn't doing so well. We weren't the only house he had to stop at that night. He had union reps who said they'd go and break the news, but he turned them all down. Nick said he took them in there, got them killed, and that he was going to finish by letting them all know what had happened."

Chuck nodded, rubbing his hands through his hair as he looked around the apartment filled with memories, pictures, and reminders. He pushed up off the couch, grabbing a micro craft beer from the fridge. He laughed at it as he was walking past.

"The least they could do was have a light beer in the fridge for dear old dad."

"We can stop and buy you a six pack on the way home, Chuck."

"I have beer at home, dear, that doesn't do me any good here though. I guess I'm going to have to try and force myself to drink-"

He stopped talking, looking down at more papers sitting on the table. He picked one up that stuck out to him, showing past due, end of service termination ninety days past due. When he picked it up he started reading it.

"What is it, hon?"

"Nothing, I just....I don't know."

"Well, get it done so you can help me out here."

"Yeah I will, quick as I can."

Chuck took the papers with him staring at the past due notices and trying to think why he cared. He kept staring at the one for the truck until it finally hit home. He took Rosa's cell phone and headed outside out of earshot. He dialed Nick from memory and after a few rings got an answer.

"Good morning to you, my beautiful Rosa. How are you doing?"

"Quit hitting on my wife, you old shit. You probably can't even get it up anymore."

Nick laughed. "Oh great it's you. Good morning to you, sweetheart. What can I do for you?"

"I have a question for you, I'm over cleaning stuff up at Traci and Isaac's house."

"Sure. I'm still working on some reports but if you give me like a half hour I will swing by, and we can do everything you need help with. I know how it is with you old guys trying to lift things."

"You're just a riot. I had a question from what you had told me when you were leaving to head to the state park."

"Look Chuck...brother, you need to try not to think about that. It isn't going to do any good for you."

"No, but it's really bugging me. Didn't you say that the detective, what's his name?"

"Detective Hardin is his name. Why, what is it?"

"Didn't you say that he had some buddies with the LoJack Company?"

"Yeah, he's always able to get answers quicker than anyone when we need information on it. I'm pretty sure he sends some amber colored liquor to a guy in customer service there on a regular basis. Why? What is it, Chuck?"

"I'm looking at Isaac's bills trying to make sense of both of their debts, and there is a bill from Kia here saying he hasn't made payment on the service in the last four months. It says that as of March it was turned off...the LoJack that is. How the hell did he find them so quick if it wasn't working?"

Nick sat forward thinking about this and knowing sometimes just because they said that they would turn the stuff off didn't mean that it had happened.

"I'll make a few calls and see what's up. He left pretty shortly after everything had ended. He said that his wife was ready for him to be done with the badge and to start doing private work. She wanted him out before it was too late to get his head fixed and put this past him. This was his second-"

Lambert trailed off, thinking about that, seeing some things that didn't make sense.

"Chuck, you finish up what you are doing. I'll get back to you later, okay?"

"Are you going to get back to me, Nick?"

"Look, I said that I would. You keep doing your job, and you let me do mine, okay? I need some time. This stuff isn't too quick and it might take me a while."

"Seems funny that he just left right after getting done with this case, doesn't it, Nick?"

"You take care of your daughter's affairs, and let me take care of this. I won't let you down. I'll make some calls until I get what I need to know."

Chapter 27

Lambert set the phone down in the cradle slowly, sitting back in his leather chair and thinking. He knew the shit storm from this would make headlines across the country. He didn't need Chuck to try and spell it out for him, he wasn't stupid. He hit his speakerphone.

"Hey, Sara, do you think that I could bug you for a favor?"

"You can ask anything you want, sugar, but whether or not I agree to do it is on a completely different story. What'cha need?"

"I want to see phone records for Hardin, am I able to do that?"

"Sure, but it isn't going to do any good if you caught him using the company line for anything but work related purposes. Besides he's gone and has already forgotten about this place. You're just wasting your time and breathe making the call."

"Well, I've heard more than once that I am full of hot air and let me worry about if I'm wasting the taxpayer's time and money."

"Do you need something to eat, Chief?"

"No, not that I know of. Why?"

"Well, you sound just a little grumpy. Do you need a Snickers? I love those commercials."

"Sara, just get me the damn files. This is pretty important to me."

"I'll order us some sandwiches; you want roast beef or chicken?"

"Damn it, I want the files!"

"You are gonna get them Chief Lambert, but you are going to get lunch too. You don't need to be all grumpy with me. I'm not afraid to call Tricia and tell her how you are treating people in your office."

Lambert did his best to control his anger, treating the receiver as if it was her neck and trying to choke it out. With clenched teeth he said. "I'll take chicken with a dill pickle and barbeque chips thank you very much, Sara."

"What flavor pie you want?"

"Cherry, please. Chocolate if that is gone."

"Now see, doesn't it feel good to be nice, Chief?"

"Oh, it's wonderful Sara, and thank you for helping me with my grumpy ways. You are just short of an angel."

"I know. Thanks, Chief. You check your email, and I'll have links for the cell phone and the office phone. You can follow them and find whatever it is you are looking for. I'll tell Evans Diner to get a move on. Diane is a mover and a shaker, she'll probably have her husband on the way here in a few minutes."

"Well, that would just be splendid." Lambert hit the end button and started hitting the refresh key every few minutes on his email browser until a new message popped up from Sara that had the links he'd requested. He clicked on the cell phone, and then the house phone for the office. He was tilting his head back and forth trying to put everything together. He knew the answers he needed were going to be severe and their end result would be extremely serious. He couldn't just make any assumptions and looked up the Kia dealer in the next county over. He got the phone number directly from the owner for who they used for LoJack service and the one that would be on Isaac's SUV.

Lambert punched in the number, waiting and pushing through the options. When he finally got through to a customer service agent he said, "I need to speak to someone about a LoJack system please."

"Can I please have your name?" The customer service representative asked.

"Yes, the account would be under Isaac Hunter. I am calling on his behalf."

"Are you a relative or a power of attorney, sir?"

"No ma'am, I'm a police chief in Missouri. I'm calling on a case, and I was hoping you would be able to give me some information that might help me solve a case that is in question."

"Sir, you would have to get verbal authorization from the owner of the account. I apologize for the inconvenience, but it is company policy."

"Did you not hear me when I said that I am the chief of police?"

"I heard you just fine sir, but unfortunately if you can't get me verbal authorization to signed information then I'm not able to answer anything for you."

"Well, it would be just a little bit difficult to be able to get authorization for that, ma'am. Do you have a supervisor that I might be able to speak to please?"

"We have to determine it truly is a supervisor matter, sir, before transferring."

Lambert kicked his drawer with the heel of his cowboy boot, crashing in the cheap plywood and feeling a bit better about it.

"The reason that I am unable to get you this verbal authorization you need so bad is because the man is dead.

185

He had a truck hood decapitate him. So for him to call you would truly be a damn miracle. Is that good enough for your dumb ass to get me to a supervisor?"

"I don't like your tone very much, sir."

"Well, I don't appreciate your fucking inability to be useful. The longer we talk, the more your existence on Earth is actually beginning to bug me. There were deaths, it was horrible, if you read the paper you'd probably already know where I am calling from."

"Oh God, you aren't calling from Missouri are you?"

"Yup, I sure as hell am."

"Fuck me. I mean, please hold, I'll transfer you to my manager, Mr. Fox."

Lambert leaned forward in his chair, writing down the chain of people he was talking to. When Fox came on he sounded like he had definitely been advised of who he was talking to.

"For lack of a better term, sir, I'd like to say good afternoon to you. How many I assist you?"

"Well, it wouldn't take too much work for you to be more helpful than that stupid shit that was on the phone with me first. I mean. Jesus good lord, were you scraping the bottom of the barrel on hiring day?"

"Unfortunately, if you saw what they paid customer service reps here, sir, you probably would be a hell of a lot more impressed at the service you got. For most people working here they'd have to improve to be referred to as stupid."

"That doesn't fill me with a lot of hope, sir. I'm trying to figure out a termination date of service on a customer of yours that I am confident missed enough bills that you shut off his service."

"Sir, we give ample warnings before shutting-"

"I'm not calling to bitch about it. I simply need the date, it is a very important matter I'm calling about. The quicker you could do things the better. Like I told the other woman, the man's name I am inquiring about is Isaac Hunter out of Missouri, if that helps narrow things down."

Lambert heard the tap tap tap of keys on the other end and just as he thought his patience was going to disappear for the rest of the day, he got a response back over the phone.

"No, primarily we give people 3 months. Now this man didn't opt for any additional features which this is one of them. Since he neglected to get any, his service has been gone since January 2000."

"So even if another police officer would have called, say two weeks ago, there would be absolutely no way whatsoever they would have received any information about a LoJack unit on that man's vehicle?"

"No sir, you miss a bill they shut it off. You go past the warning date, which was months ago, and you are done. That LoJack unit is just a paperweight at this point."

"I see. Okay, Mr. Fox, I thank you very much. You have a good day."

"Good luck with your investigation, Chief Lambert."

"I...I will, thank you." Lambert set the phone back down in the cradle. He looked up to see Sara standing there watching him.

"Is there something that I can do for you, Sara?"

"You can tell me what's really wrong."

Lambert smiled uneasily and she could almost see his

face turning green. He leaned over, grabbed his wastebasket, and lost everything he had eaten that morning, which for once he was thankful that he had skipped the big breakfast option over coffee.

"You know I think that I'm going to go home. I am pretty sure I have some sort of a bug. I think the last few weeks have really gotten to me."

"Yes, sir, that seems like quite a good idea. You go on home, there ain't nothing you need to worry about being done today, sir. Besides, you got that murdering son of a bitch off the streets at least you can sleep at night now, right?"

"Yeah, thank you Sara. I think I might be out tomorrow as well."

Chapter 28

Lambert climbed into his pickup truck and sat in the driver's seat holding the keys in his hand. He had a moral dilemma, one that was seriously splitting him in half. He had taken an oath, one that made him uphold the laws. At the same time, he could not decide how he could not give his friend the news that the killer was still alive. That the man that had taken his daughter from him had received awards for his valor and recognition for his bravery all across America.

He turned the key over, driving slowly at first until he was racing down the highway towards his home. He stopped quickly in the driveway, scaring Tricia half to death in the window. Lambert went inside not saying anything. He went to his closet, ignoring Tricia doing her best not to be nosy while standing in the doorway.

"Well, hello to you too, Chief Lambert. It's been awhile since you've came home for a nooner."

Lambert turned around, seeing his wife in an apron, fully dressed, and shaking her stuff for him, mocking him.

"I wish that was why I was here. I did some research on a case, and it's going to end up making me need to travel for a few days. Do you think that you'll be okay for a couple days by yourself?"

"Since when have you ever had to go somewhere for your job?"

"Honey, I just finished wrapping up a national case and I looked up some additional information for someone. Needless to say something got overlooked. I just need to go and give some depositions, and I will be back before you miss me."

Tricia laughed. "I don't know dear, it might take longer than you think. I mean as much as I appreciate picking up dirty underwear off of the floor and having a heart attack at two in the morning when I need to go pee and almost falling into the toilet, I think it could take a day or two."

"You'll miss me, baby. You don't have to say it just so poetically as you do."

Nick pulled out his bag, slid a few pairs of work uniforms in and a few pairs of jeans.

"Do you need any help packing, Nicky?"

"Nope, you make me a thermos of coffee, and I'll be heading out. They said they'd get me a room to stay up in Iowa. Some town just outside of Des Moines named Ankeny I'm going to stay in. I need the caffeine, and maybe a sandwich to make it up there without falling asleep."

"I'll make you two. I don't want you crashing that truck out in the middle of nowhere. If your cell phone or CB radio doesn't work, then you'll have a hell of a time walking to the nearest small town."

Lambert was just barely able to have a conversation that made sense, said, "Sure honey, thanks for doing that. I appreciate it."

She disappeared and when she was gone he pulled out a pistol that he'd gotten from a swap meet quite a few years back and slid it and the ammunition for it into his travel bag. He grabbed his shaving kit and toiletries from the bathroom. He gave his wife a hug, one that was long and hard, before he left. She pushed him out just a foot from her and looked him in the eyes.

"Nick, is there anything that you want to tell me before you leave? I'm used to you being weird, but you are being extra weird today."

"Yeah, the last few weeks haven't been easy on me. I'll get back to normal, just give me some time. It isn't easy, okay? This last week messed with my head."

"Well, you get back to normal. You have too many friends and family and employees that look to you. We can't have you losing your mind after all this, okay?"

Lambert gave her a kiss on the forehead and one last squeeze before heading out to the truck. She watched him and could see in his eyes that there was more going on than he could tell her. She hoped for her sake that he would at the very least be safe and come back to her in one piece and a healthy state of mind.

Lambert drove like a robot. He had so many things running wildly through his mind that he didn't realize that he'd driven to Chuck's house and not to Traci and Isaac's apartment. When he made it to the apartment he sat out in his truck for ten minutes before going up there. He had never been a vigilante, had worked hard for what he had gotten in life. Lambert knew sometimes people would get away with crimes. He thought about Colorado, Iowa where he was now, and Missouri, and to his knowledge they did not have the death penalty. The visuals of Traci being decimated by that bomb and shotgun blast didn't seem as if a cushy matte with a few needles taped to his arm would seem justified. He had never been a man who believed in torturing another, but at the same time he'd been a God fearing man going to church his entire life. There was one thing he knew God believed in and that was do unto others

191

as you wish to have done to you. He thought about Hardin and thought that yes he did deserve it. He was a disease and he needed to be eradicated. He knew Chuck was hard, but didn't know if justice like this was something he would pursue. Lambert was pretty confident if that meant they knew who did it he surely would though.

Lambert put his truck in park, then slid out and walked slowly up the steps. When he made it to the doorway it was already open and he saw Rosa in there wiping at her eyes as two men from Goodwill stacked boxes on a dolly and took what seemed like a never-ending row of items no longer needed downstairs. When she saw Lambert she walked over.

"Oh hey Nick, you didn't need to come all the way over here. We got a good handle on things. Don't tell me Chuck actually forgot to bring something with him. Not that his head might of been a little foggy when we left."

"Hey, Rosa, no…he didn't forget anything. I just wanted to have a quick chat with him. You think he has a minute for me?"

"Yeah, anyone else I might say no, but I think he'll be happy to see you."

Lambert walked by, squeezing her arm and thinking how he needed to go tell his absolute one true friend in the entire world how the man that killed his daughter had been hired by him. How he had been paying the man who had been on a murdering rampage to find the killer. He thought how this was almost a fucking stand-up joke, be it for the mentally twisted, but he could be looked at as the fucking stupidest police chief in the United States. The one thing that ran through his mind was that Hardin hadn't been in

Iowa long enough for him to begin killing. He thought if they took him out, or if just he if Chuck was not up for it, everyone could just continue thinking that it was the person blown up in the woods.

Lambert tapped on the door outside, watching Chuck swearing under his breath about some China made piece of damn shit on the floor. He looked up.

"I said, that I'd tell you when it was ready and that no. I did not need no damn,"

He saw that it was Lambert there trying to smile but looked like he had come to deliver the worst news he possibly could. Chuck dropped the tool.

"What, what is it?"

Lambert shook his head no, he didn't want to say it at first but broke down.

"Not here, come on. I got a feeling you'll be thinking this is important, or at the very least you'll want a hand in this. You need to come up with something saying that I need you to help me do a quick drive for some information that needs to be heard from a witness's mouth, but I'm half sick, and you are going to drive me there. All expenses paid."

"Why the hell would you need me to drive you somewhere? Christ, are you getting that old?"

Nick pulled up his shirt, he'd tucked the gun in his belt after leaving. He showed off the revolver that definitely was not his service piece. "Because you and I have some unfinished business that we need to put to bed, brother."

"Did you find something?"

"Again if you don't want to break her heart all over again, I suggest highly, that we head outside and have a chat, but save yourself the trip back up those stairs. I'll lay down the lie for you. You just take it home okay?"

Chuck nodded, and within five minutes he was walking down the stairs with a purpose. He climbed into Nick's pickup and said, "Okay spill it. Spill all of it."

"I took your tip like you said about the LoJack because it was a helluva great question. I checked, and they said it had been off for months. I went a few steps further though, and Hardin never made any calls to the number where you would check it; no one from the office did that day. I saw the only call he made that day was to us to call in backup. Apparently he had plans to make a blood bath out of it, or he would have just done them on Saturday when he had the opportunity."

Chuck laid his head back shaking it. "This is fucking crazy. So what, you want to drive up there and kill him? Is that something that you can live with?"

"It wouldn't be the first time I've killed someone, Chuck."

"War doesn't count. We were told repeatedly that we were going to fight the enemy. By the time we made it over there, we half thought Vietnam belonged to us and they should thank us for invading their country. I don't want you jeopardizing your job and your life that you've built. I know you worked your ass off to get where you are. We both have, and the one thing we need to ask also is, can we live with our decisions if something goes wrong and we get caught?"

Lambert looked over at him. "I don't think I can go on living knowing I was basically living with a killer for all those months. All the pity we felt for that sick son of a bitch having to be a lone wolf out there hunting the killer. All the hours he was putting in and the families he had to talk to. Jesus Christ, he probably gave himself a fucking hard on getting to see their faces. He probably ate it up on the way there, during, and after. I don't need to think about anything. I simply wanted to make sure you had the option. I'm not going to deprive you of justice and if you want a hand in it, then you can do it. If you simply want to stay here with Rosa and know things are being handled then you won't be judged by-"

"No, I'm going. Skip my house. I can buy clothes up there if I need to."

Lambert didn't want to be a stickler, but he said, "You might want to get a change of clothes, honestly."

"Why, is that?"

"Because you are going to look a little suspicious going into a store soaked in blood covered clothes. I also want to hit up your garage and grab a few shovels. Just make sure you get the ones that you don't care if we don't bring back with us."

"There isn't anything that I care about as much as that girl. I'm fine using whatever I have to use to put closure to this. It's just a shame that we won't ever be able to tell Rosa the truth."

Lambert looked at him. "I don't know what good it is going to do knowing this. I think if anything I'll be worse off for it. The only thing that will make me feel the least bit better is the simple fact that the son of a bitch won't be able to get a taste going again for the kill. I think he's smart enough to know when it's time to get out of an area. If I had to make a guess, I'd say the man from Colorado was framed by Hardin, and for whatever reason, they never were able to prove him innocent."

"What do you expect, Lambert? I mean think about it, for God sakes, he knows the system inside and out. He probably planted everything to perfection and left the son of a bitch there holding the bag. He got recognition and fame for it, and that son of a bitch will look at four walls for the rest of his life."

"I will drop an anonymous message to the FBI that they need to look into this son of a bitch. I looked up his old addresses over the last twenty years, with the exception of one stint for five years there have been killings near or in all of them. There was only one that I wasn't able to see a killing at, but he was enlisted in the Air Force back then as a bomb technician. You want to guess if the local city saw a blood fest during that time?"

"I probably don't want to know, do I?"

"No, there's a pretty damn good chance that you don't want to know. This fucker loves his business and unfortunately for him, there are plenty of pickings around."

"Well, I'd think that it would be much easier for someone when they do not have any care if it is man or woman, young or old. That really opens your options up, I'd think."

"If we don't fuck up then hopefully your Traci is going to be the last one that had to suffer at his hands."

Chuck was quiet after that, and Lambert knew from the look on his face he wasn't sad, he was pissed and he was thinking in detail what it was he was going to do when he finally caught up to the son of a bitch.

"I got this gun and it's clean. We get him in the back

of the truck and we'll have no issues from there. I'm sure there are plenty of places out in the middle of nowhere that a body is never going to be found," Lambert said.

Chuck nodded slowly, tapping his fingers on his legs as he thought about it.

"As long as it hurts. It has to hurt. That piece of shit doesn't deserve any better. He doesn't deserve anything but the worst. He even showed up at the damn wake to express his concerns for how we were feeling."

"They don't call them insane for any other reason, brother. We will right the wrong or at least do as much as we can. If at any point you change your mind, or can't do it, you let me know, and we can do this the proper way. This is your call."

Chuck looked at Lambert. "We aren't changing anything. This is how it is and I'm not going to change a damn thing. All I can say is that I want the only reason we need that gun is to get him in the truck. Once we get that done the only thing I want to use on him is the knives and shovels. I plan on him experiencing a slow and painful death. I'm going to make him scream until my ears bleed and his throat runs dry and then....I'm going to cut his tongue from his mouth."

Lambert nodded. "Yep, I can live with that, Chuck. I'm just sorry I didn't figure this out beforehand."

"Stop apologizing. That is like you thinking someone in the marines would have been on the Vietnamese side back in Nam, man. You don't suspect it, you don't question it, because he is supposed to be the man that you can turn around and know that he has your six. I just don't understand it, but I don't think that either one of us ever will."

"Well, Chuck, it definitely doesn't do anything to make my heart hurt any less, man. She was such a sweet fucking kid. God, it makes me just want to do things to that man that are indescribable."

"Well, they should be imaginable at the very least once you are done doing it to him."

Chapter 29

Evening Ankeny, Iowa

Lambert had pulled up near the Hardin residence a half hour ago. The two men had been sitting there waiting to see if someone was home and if they were if it was Matt or not. They did not want to have any conversations with him until they were where they needed to be. Lambert saw the minivan leave with the wife in it and when she came back and no one helped her with groceries but the children an hour later that was when Lambert stepped out of the truck, making sure the gun was tucked under his shirt and out of sight, but ready to be pulled. "Let's go see if they are just as friendly when visitors drop in."

"You sure you don't want to wait out here?"

"No, if he comes home he's going to have us there waiting for him. I think if the wife knows we are waiting around at some point she's going to see us and make a report to the police. I can't imagine how paranoid the poor woman has to be knowing that, or at least thinking that, her husband was the man that went after killers. I would hate to think that any serial killer would want to track me down just to make a name for himself. You know, to be able to say that you took out the man that tried to take the Stranger down."

"You are the one who knows about this shit. You just tell me what you need me to do, Lambert, and I'll be on your side. I really, really appreciate you doing this for me. You could have let it go. You could have let it be someone else's problem, and just called the police letting the information be handled by someone else and letting him go through the process."

"Well, I'm pretty sure that with someone like this, if they decided to plead insanity there wouldn't be a really big issue about getting that plea to stick. The last thing I want is for him to live a cushy life for the next thirty to forty years inside a room painting pictures and pissing himself because he is so doped up."

Chuck shuddered at the idea the man would be allowed to live, and they climbed the steps, rapping on the door four times until a little boy answered wearing what looked like last year's Halloween costume. Hardin's wife, Jamie, came to the door, pushing the boy back, yelling his full name, and he turned around running for safety.

"God, you'd think with a father who was a police officer that you wouldn't open the door for strangers for God's sake. You should thank the Lord we live in such a nice community now."

Lambert put on his friendly face, waving. "Well, he might have seen my badge, ma'am. You remember me? I think we met at the funerals. My name is-"

"Chief Lambert, how are you? Is everything okay?"

"Peachy, Mrs. Hardin, I just happened to be in the county for a convention and me and my buddy thought we'd swing in and see how Matt was doing. Thought maybe we'd take him out for a cold one with some of that hard-earned money the state gives me to spend while we are away. I don't know if you've met my good friend, Chuck Pendergrast?"

"No, I don't think that I have...." She covered her face. "Oh my God, that young woman, that was your daughter, wasn't it? Oh my, I'm so sorry that happened. I can't tell you how relieved I was to hear the son of a bitch got taken out. He deserves to burn in hell for the rest of his days. I mean, you can't trust anyone nowadays."

Chuck smiled uneasily. "Yes, well, thank you for those kind words. I am glad it was taken care of as well. I would have hated to see the killer go to trial only to have them get a not guilty plea."

Lambert cut in saying. "So are we lucky enough to be able to catch Matt, sweetheart?"

"No, you know what, it seems like the further he tries to get away from police work the more hours it is he needs to work. He said the resources just aren't what they were when he was on the force. He is really having to put in some serious time around this new job though just to get up and running with it. The last guy they had he said messed things up so badly you couldn't make hide nor hair of what it was they were trying to do on a daily basis."

"You mind if we wait inside for him?"

"I would be happy to let you in, but this was just one errand on a list of many we got going. I can check and see when he's going to be home if you want?"

"No, you don't need to call and bug him."

"Who's calling? I got this nifty thing on my phone and all I gots to do is hit 'find Matt' on this little GPS tracker and it shows me where he is within about twenty feet. You can't get any smarter than this here thing."

She stared at it for a few moments and then started to laugh. "Oh my, I can't believe that."

"Ma'am?" Lambert asked.

"Oh, he always forgets his stupid phone at home.

Says right here that he is already home. He only remembers his head I think because the damn thing is attached."

Lambert held out his hand to shake hers.

"Well, don't you worry then. Maybe we can swing by his employer and see if he wants to go out. Just seems a shame coming all this way and not getting a chance to catch up with him."

"Well, I'll be sure to let him know that I saw you if you men don't run him down first."

Chuck smiled, thinking about this. "Well, we can certainly hope can't we?"

"Well, good luck to you both."

Chapter 30

Chuck and Nick waved as Jamie pulled out of the driveway with the kids in tow. Chuck said, "Christ, he doesn't have his cell phone. Do you think he might be out doing it right now? I would think he'd have to give it some time before he could start out, people would start thinking eventually that there is a pretty fat fucking coincidence, right?"

Lambert looked up, shaking his head. "I would like to tell you no, but I sure as hell don't consider myself ignorant, and the fact that happened in my county the two things never dawned on me. You know if it wasn't for all the killing and loss there is something that would actually be funny to me."

"What in the hell about any of this would be funny?"

"The fact I felt sorry for that poor son of a bitch. Each day and night I woke up feeling bad for what he was going through and went to bed feeling the same damn thing. I thought, you know if there was another job I had to do if I wasn't Chief, I would not want his job and it didn't matter what you paid me. I came back from 'Nam and I could have lived out the rest of my existence living a meager, unentertaining life."

"Yeah, I can't say turning wrenches after I put down my gun was a stressful job at all. I was just fine, and I knew kind of like you there'd always be crime, where for me there'd always be someone needing something fixed. So what do we do now, sit here all fucking night until that piece of shit comes home?"

"That, or we can go get a bite to eat so we can sit

here watching with a full belly."

"I really can't say for sure that right now I'll be able to eat."

"Me either, just didn't want you starving until he comes home. I know how you old timers get when you don't get any food in you."

"You know god damn well, Lambert, that I'm only three months older than you."

"Well, from what Rosa said to Tricia, those are three important months."

Chuck stared at Lambert for a minute across the hood. He knew these were fabricated lies and after a minute his face finally broke free into a genuine smile filled with mischief. "Sorry, I couldn't help myself. Come on, we are going to get the cops called on us sitting out here with Missouri plates in the middle of an upper class neighborhood like this."

The two climbed in. "I don't know, this place isn't screaming with activity on the street." Chuck said.

The masked man appeared from the backseat before either of them could say anything. He held a pistol in each hand to the back of their skulls.

"That's why we like it here. It's quiet boys."

Both men screamed when the man appeared. The stranger said. "Pull out your pistol, Chief. I want to see it with your index and thumb only."

Lambert complied by reaching in and sending three shots from it into the back seat. The stranger screamed, going back in his seat and grabbing his side. Chuck looked over. "You got the son of a-"

Lambert's brains and skull painted the left inside of

the truck. A single bullet exploded through the window, which was covered with bits of black and gray hair. His blood and brains slowly rolled out of the large hole from the side of his head resting on his shoulder.

Lambert let out a final breath, leaning forward. The stranger looked down, seeing the blood coming from his side. He was unsure if it was life threatening at the moment, but knew that by the grace of God, or maybe more accurately the devil, the bullet had gone in and out and would be one thing later to answer for.

Chuck screamed, in rage. His emotions were on fire and he had no wish to extinguish them.

"Oh my god, Nick, Nick, oh fuck, I'm gonna cut your fucking insides out with a spoon, you piece of shit!"

"Now that's the spirit. How are you doing by the way? Is the fact that your daughter had her head blown off and then got to have most of her remains put into a Ziploc bag gotten easier?"

"I don't have to deal with this. I don't have to answer anything."

The stranger sat forward in his seat. "You still live at 555 Nightvale Lane, right? You live there with your lovely wife Rosa? Let me ask, sir, were you her first? I guess maybe more important, do you think you will be her last?"

"If you touch my wife!"

"Relax, it isn't my thing. I get aroused by ripping people's guts out, hearing those sweet, sweet screams. Some are better than others of course, but you probably know what I mean. Let's go for a spin. We can't have the truck still sitting out here, after multiple gunshots. This is a nice neighborhood, and my wife really likes it. Do me a favor and scoot Chief Lambert out of the way, and let's have us a little drive. I tell you what, why don't we head out to a nice park? I always make new friends."

"I'm not going to chauffeur you to your next kill."

"You will, or I'm going to shoot you now, drive myself down to Missouri with your two dead bodies riding shotgun, and kill Nick's wife, his children, and his grandchildren. And then I'm going to kill your wife, Rosa, but I'm going to skin her alive and send her naked, hairless body out to die in the street in front of everyone."

Chuck opened his mouth to speak. He couldn't even visualize what he was saying. "You're sick."

"Noted, now get Nicky out of the way and slide into the driver's seat. I'm sure that police were called after the first gunshot. I can only imagine there are fifty sets of nosy eyes on us at this very moment."

Chuck awkwardly slid Nick to his seat, climbed over him, and sat in the driver's seat, feeling the seat squish under him and knowing what it was. The wetness he felt wasn't something that made him feel good. Chuck put the truck in gear and pulled away slowly.

"You take it nice and easy. Don't go doing anything stupid, like getting in a crash on purpose. I'm a big guy and young, I'll survive, and you won't."

"You pull out on to Highway 69 here and head north for about five miles. We'll end up out at Big Creek State Park. They have camping and a beach; it's really quite lovely. I went there with the kids so they could play, and it was all I could do not to pull out my machete and just chop all those little delicious families into pieces right there."

"I knew you weren't retired. I knew that you weren't

done."

"Why would I quit? Do you know how wonderful this is? I love my life, Chuck. I couldn't be happier and more fulfilled. Do you know how rare it is nowadays to be able to say that?"

Chuck drove, almost missing the turn, but Hardin saw it and pistol-whipped him across the rear of the head.

"Turn here. Do it now."

"What's with the mask? If you are just going to kill them, what point does it have, what purpose?"

"Oh, Chuck, masks are fun. Do you know this is probably the first conversation I've ever got to have with someone...before I killed them that is. The mask is scary."

He got up close behind Chuck, putting a hand over his chest and keeping the gun to his temple.

"Do you feel that? Do you? Oh my God that is ecstasy to me. Now, I like to think I'm kind of a looker, so if I just came out with a machete as scary as a giant like me would be, I think it would lose something, don't you?"

Chuck nodded slowly, feeling his heart racing, and wished he'd just have a damn heart attack going fifty-five miles per hour down the highway. Chuck nodded because he really did see what he was talking about.

"So what, you drive us out there, bury us and then take the truck somewhere to be disposed of?"

"You know that is going to be just a bit tricky now. You went and ruined my plans getting me shot. I'm going to have to go kill some unlucky bystander in the ghetto neighborhood in Des Moines now and give them Nicky boy's gun there so everything matches up. Not going to go well with my current employer, but I'm sure they'll be more than understanding about it. I mean, I'll be a hero killing the bad guy, off duty, weeks after giving up the badge, pampered by all and pitied by the wife for my pain."

Chuck could see the campsite and since it was midweek it wasn't very full. He knew he couldn't bring his problems to these people. He thought of Rosa doing the sign of the cross. Hardin saw this.

"Don't do anything stupid, Chuck."

"We should have just called the cops. We had all the evidence we needed to at the least open up a floodgate worth of investigations heading your way."

Hardin went to say something and Chuck pulled the wheel to the left, sending the truck down into a ditch where it came back up looking like it was going to just drive right up the other side. Chuck pulled the wheel all the way to the left, sending the truck and it's three occupants bouncing around like ping pong balls, a bloody one mind you in the case of Lambert, until it skidded to a stop not twenty feet from the first camper.

Chuck was breathing heavy. He looked around when the truck came to a rest, feeling a sharp pain from the back of his lower abdomen. He looked down and saw in the crash the gearshift knob had somehow broken off. What was left of the rod was protruding through and out the back of Chuck's torso. He looked in the back, stuck where he was in place. "Oh thank god, he's dead."

The mask came back up slowly; blood was dripping from behind the mask down onto his shirt. The stranger shook his head no and pulled up a machete for Chuck to see. The stranger drew a smiley face on his cheek and took the blade slowly, very slowly, an inch at a time, up Chuck's abdomen and towards his neck, not stopping until his wrist was buried within his stomach. Blood began to pour from his mouth and all he could do was think of Rosa. "I'm sorry Rosa, I'm so sorry."

The stranger put a finger to his lips, shushing him, and whispered, "No, but you will be."

Chapter 31

That night

The busty blonde stood out in front of the scene. She held the mic up as the man counted down four, three, two, and go to her. She held up the mic. "Good evening, this is KCCI News Channel 8 here first. We got an anonymous tip less than an hour ago and were able to meet up with police on the scene. They are not saying anything, but from first look, I think there is a new killer on the loose. There are two Missouri residents who are yet to be identified. We looked at the truck and other than a Missouri sticker on the bumper there are no identifying marks. We saw the victims being removed from the truck and their hands and heads had been removed. When police went to local campers, they were unable to find anyone available to question. Now within the last hour police have shown up in droves and have been scouring the woods looking for the killer, but all they have been able to find are the temporary residents of the campsite. I overheard a few deputies saying this screams of the slaughtering that took place in Missouri not more than a month ago, which shook the nation when the news came out that they were finally able to put an end to the killings. Now the question is was this a copycat killing, or did the killer truly get away down south and make his way here to this safe and peaceful campsite? We will have more details as they come to us, but as of now the police are not releasing any information. This is Leslie Bryant with Channel 8 and I'll be locking my doors and windows twice tonight."

Chapter 32

Sunday of the search

Christy screamed as best she could as she heard the police sirens echoing in the deep distance. She started to cry uncontrollably when she saw Detective Hardin's head come up over the edge of the steps. She was shaking, not even caring at the nails pulling at her feet and hands. She had a smile only a mother could love as it was intertwined with the yarn and blood keeping it shut. Matt hushed her, coming to kneel before her. He smiled, but not a smile that was meant to calm her. He took off his police jacket, exposing a rig with the mask and a machete both dangling from his sides. "Now you didn't expect me to forget about you, did you?"

Chapter 33

Near future

The man used his cane to walk up the path to the old home. It was dark and the grass was overgrown; there had been no one to care for it recently since Chuck's passing. The man pushed the doorbell twice, waiting patiently. A woman answered, the man said, "Hello, Rosa, Rosa Pendergrast?"

To be continued

Written by Mike Evans

A quick note from the author, if you enjoyed this please head to Amazon to REVIEW or give it a star rating please. The sequel is ready for you to preorder/order!!

Discover other titles by Mike Evans visit Amazon

The Orphans Series
The Orphans: Origins Vol I
Surviving the Turned Vol II (The Orphans Series)
Strangers Vol III (The Orphans Series)
White Lie Vol IV (The Orphans Series)
Civil War Vol V (The Orphans Series)

Zombies and Chainsaws
Zombies and Chainsaws 1
Dark Roads (Zombies and Chainsaws 2)

The Rising Series
Deal with the Devil Book 1

Gabriel Series
Gabriel: Only one gets out alive
Pitch Black (Gabriel Book 2)
Body Count (Gabriel Book 3)

The Uninvited Series
The Uninvited Book 1
The Stranger Book II of The Uninvited series coming soon

Buried: Broken oaths